DISRAELI HALL

DISRAELI HALL

Sue Knight

First Published 2020 by
Fantastic Books Publishing

ISBN (eBook): 978-1-914060-04-5
ISBN (paperback): 978-1-914060-02-1
ISBN (large print): 978-1-914060-03-8

Better is a dish of vegetables where there is love than a fattened bull where there is hatred.

Proverbs 15:17

DEDICATION

To my parents Jan and Margaret, and my granny Margaret, with love

CHAPTER 1

Darkness had crept into Disraeli Hall. It had filtered through the corridors of the empty servants' quarters and had begun to cloud the corners of the library, where Sarah worked on oblivious. She moved another pile of yellowing documents from her in-tray to filing and paused for a moment, caught by the beauty of the gardens, illuminated by the low sun.

The view from the massive library windows was always lovely. Always. Even at that bleak moment of early February, where the black earth showed in patches through the skeleton of January snow. She had sat there through all the seasons, processions of them. She had arrived on a rainy Spring evening, and awoken to the glory of new green. And it had ended here, at the tag end of Winter. Wasn't there a word, or an expression; pathetic fallacy? Something like that? Where the weather, or the natural world, was in perfect sympathy with the plot?

It certainly fitted her story. She had arrived here so full of hope, a new life beginning. And it was ending like this. A servant where once she was Chatelaine! How dramatic that sounded. As if she were an unfortunate young lady in a Jane Austen ... no, it would be a Victorian novel surely – a Mrs Henry Wood. The Misfortunes of Sarah Cavalier. No. Mrs Cavalier's Troubles.

Well, get on with your cataloguing, Sarah, she scolded herself. She needed the money. That was one of her troubles. And Clifford certainly wouldn't pay her for sitting around. There was nothing Victorian about him. He was very much a high tech man. And she didn't think she could hope that he, as the new Lord of the Manor, was going to recognize her sterling qualities and take her away from all this to be his bride. If he did, that would be pure Mills and Boon, wouldn't it? And where would his young Sloaney wife fit into the picture?

This had been Sarah's favourite room when she first came here. There was no information superhighway here then. Just walls of old books, with their cosy smell. She used to sit at the massive windows, looking out over the formal garden, imagining herself the second Mrs De Winter. There she was, at Manderley. Only, unlike its anonymous heroine, she had a name. She was Sarah. Sarah Cavalier.

She could almost see the gardens in their full Spring glory. The plans they had! She and Leo were going to … The vivid sun, uninterrupted by the skeletal trees, shone its farewell right into her eyes. Her watch shocked her. Where had the afternoon gone? It'd be getting dark in no time. The sun was so low on the horizon. Even Maggs would have left.

And Mrs Maggs would be long gone. Nobody stayed at Disraeli Hall after dark now.

Sarah began to switch off computers and unplug things. Come on, come on, machines, hurry yourselves up, she bustled impatiently at them. Shadows were dark in the corners of the library. Night had flooded in behind her while she was lulled by the brightness of the setting sun.

But all the precious documents and books had to be carefully stacked away. Though there were few of them now. As they were scanned and catalogued, they were disappearing into the vault. Clifford considered the library to be an unsuitable and unscientific place to keep valuable old books and papers.

In fact he, Clifford Cavalier Betts, the last – or was it the latest? – of the Cavaliers, found Disraeli Hall itself unscientific, unsuitable and generally unsatisfactory, and was emphatically doing something about it. Sarah was a small cog in the wheel of his library plans.

Clifford's arrival, to claim his inheritance, had made her feel for a moment that she was a protagonist in a different sort of story altogether. The Canterville Ghost. Had there been a family ghost, had there been such things as ghosts. Because no ghost could have survived Clifford. He could rationalize anything away. The library was clean of books, as the grounds were going to become clean of the tall, old trees. And the rambling moorland approach to the house was being replaced by a clean-cut drive that would lead straight to the Tramway.

Disraeli Hall, soon to become Hotel, was being swept clean so that it could host The Benjamin Disraeli Experience. Facts about the great man would fill the library – on interactive machines. Never had he been so catalogued, so dissected.

Never had such information been gathered about him, from the labelling of every chair he might have sat in to the tiniest detail of his politics.

But something had been exorcised after all: Benjamin Disraeli himself. The feeling Sarah had had of his once-presence here on that fleeting but fateful visit. Her sense that the past was not as distant as we thought, that it impinged on the present at every moment. That had gone. And it had taken with it Sarah's last feeling of regret at the loss of Disraeli Hall.

Finally, everything was safely put away, switched off, sealed in. Sarah shivered. The library, never warm, was chilling down rapidly as the sun went. She looked round. How dark it was. She wished she could let herself out through the French windows and just leave via the gardens, although they would be getting dark now. Anyway, she couldn't. The windows were locked and she no longer had the key. She would just have to let herself out the back, by the servants' entrance. No problem. Or was she now as nervous of the night as any old-fashioned Victorian heroine? Was that all that marriage to Leo had done for her?

Oh, and she must make sure to set the downstairs alarms. Derek Maggs would have done the rest. It was oddly frightening to set an alarm in a dark house. When you knew you were on your own. All sorts of horrible possibilities ...

Come on, Sarah, lights off. Computers off. Everything put away. French windows locked. Alarms set. Sarah looked back into the room, her hand on the light switch, and fought an impulse to go and check the window locks. She knew they were locked. They were locked when she arrived. She hadn't touched them, and no one had been in the library apart from her. Not even Ava

Maggs, making a pretence of light dusting.

What was wrong with her? She never used to be like this. She used to be Sarah Dexter. Once. Right. And she would be her again. She would. She would not give in to this obsession. She was not going to turn the alarm off and check the window locks.

But the invocation to her single self failed, and Sarah was compelled to check every window, and the massive glass doors. She was startled by the darkness of the gardens.

Why did they never think to fix up some lighting out there? Well, they did of course, and they were going to restore ... No. Now was most definitely not the time to be thinking about the past. It was as if she had gone from Manderley to Hill House, via ... Another wrong train of thought, Sarah. Stop it. Now.

All done. The room was shut down, secured, safe for the night. The alarms were reset. All she had to do was to walk down the corridor to the old kitchens.

It was a low cosy corridor, part of the farmhouse that had been the beginning of Disraeli Hall many centuries ago. Quiet in its creams and browns, it had nothing of the cold splendour of the frontage. It led to the door that had been the Berlin Wall between master and servant. And beyond it was the surprise of the second staircase, which wound up to the servants' tiny bedrooms. She had thought it was such fun, finding she had a second staircase.

Sarah hesitated at the door. Come on, she rallied herself, it's getting darker by the minute. And you've to pick Annie up from the Brats' at five. Just a quick step through that pool of darkness at the bottom of the stairs and she would be inside the little scullery, with its wooden sink and constant stagnant smell. The light switch was right inside the door of the main kitchen.

Why did she never do anything about that awkward area? Why did Ava Maggs never mention it? She moaned enough about everything else. If only there was a full complement of servants. Just to hear sounds of bustling life ahead of her. And light, and a jolly cook and a scullery maid. A fierce cook and a sullen scullery maid would do. Even Mrs Danvers! Even Mrs Maggs.

Sarah nearly laughed out loud at the idea of Ava Maggs as Mrs Danvers, endlessly brooding over her lost mistress. Ava couldn't lose mistresses fast enough. 'Men are so much easier to manage' could well be a Maggsian proverb.

Laughter dispelled the fear that seemed to linger in this part of the house, and Sarah felt better. She was not leaving this light on, turning the kitchen lights on, and coming back to turn this off. She was not. That would be utterly pathetic. Next thing she'd be back in the library checking all the doors and windows again. And there would be no reason why the whole pantomime shouldn't go on all night.

Everything was locked, turned off, alarmed, fine-tuned behind her. She was turning the light off now. She was taking the few steps through the pool of darkness at the bottom of the stairs to the next light switch. Then she would be into the back kitchens and away home. There was nothing here to be afraid of.

Nothing here now, anyway.

Why did the last words she wanted to hear come into her mind at just the very moment she didn't want them there?

There was nothing to worry about. There was no one in Disraeli Hall but Sarah. And no one could get in now. There was that 'now' again, with its disturbing resonance.

No one could get in now without triggering enough noise and neon lighting to bring Maggs from the

Gatehouse and probably a fleet of police cars from the town. Clifford was a Very Important Person, after all.

Right, Sarah, she ordered herself. Take a deep breath, and go. Darkness swallowed everything up as the light clicked off. But three steps and she would be reaching for the kitchen light switch. It would be just about there.

And, instantly, paralysingly, she could feel in her palm the memory of the clicking of another light switch in the dark. The clicking and the clicking. But no light. And all the time that terrible scream ringing in her ears.

She had woken up in the dark bedroom, the scream echoing and echoing. She had grabbed for Leo, but there was no one there. Just an empty space in the bed beside her.

She had reached for the bedside light. Found the switch instantly. And clicked and clicked.

And nothing. Only darkness.

Sarah could remember the feeling of cold. She had been so cold. And the silence of the house. She shivered. She was cold now. And the house was as silent as the grave. The grave where Leo …

She had called 'Leo?' into the darkness of that night. And heard the echoes of her call fade back into the waiting silence. And then she had heard the footsteps, coming slowly up the stairs.

No. She would not think about it. She wouldn't remember it. It never happened. Never. If she didn't think about it, it didn't happen. She would get the light on and get out of dark Disraeli Hall. But her fingers were frozen, unable to reach for the switch.

Which horror was worse? Standing here in the pool of darkness where it must have happened, or trying to turn on the light and finding …

Finding what? Grow up, Sarah.

Whoever had stood there, waiting, on

the night of the scream and the footsteps that came slowly, slowly up the stairs, was waiting for Leo. Not her. They were long gone, undiscoverable apparently. Why would they come back?

And as for the dead, they don't walk. She knew that. The dead were dead. They were conscious of nothing at all. Believe that, if you won't believe anything else, Sarah.

Who had said that to her?

It had comforted her then. And it consoled and strengthened her now. She reached for the switch again.

But the second before her hand found it, the light came on.

CHAPTER 2

The Sarah of three years ago, a much, much younger Sarah, had been surprised by the isolation of the Hall. Leo had always spoken as if the Northern town had swallowed up Hall and village together in its vast urban sprawl. But she was to find that its large grounds and tall old trees still kept it solitary. To the west, its long gardens met the moor, and Sarah would watch grazing sheep, rabbits, sometimes even a stoat, as the heather came and went in its purple.

And, to isolate it further, back in the twenties, the incumbent Cavalier, outraged that someone was building a row of red brick bungalows in the village, had closed off the wide drive that had run from the Gatehouse to the imposing frontage. And so Disraeli Hall had cut itself off from its disobedient village.

Goodness knows what the old Cavaliers would say now. The Councillor Albert Cowlishaw Tramway had swept up to the yards and outhouses that backed the old servants' quarters. The trams had never arrived – there had been some problem with EU grants – but the road certainly had. The sprawl of council and private estates had encompassed the village. Only the moorland had stopped them. The Peak Park held its borders fiercely.

It had been a dramatic enough homecoming. They had driven up from London, the excitement of their whirlwind courtship, their hasty wedding, behind them. Leo had mentioned taking the scenic route, but Sarah hadn't been expecting the winding leisurely approach across the moors. In that chilly late Spring, they seemed as flat and boundless as the sea.

'Brrr.' She snuggled closer to Leo. 'I can feel the temperature dropping all the time. And look at those clouds coming up.'

He had smiled his radiant smile at her. 'I'll have to go out and shoot a bear for you, you soft Southerner. You can hibernate in its furs through what we call Summer up here. We'll Winter in Sorrento or somewhere.'

'Ok, that'll do me. Providing you hibernate beside me.'

His hair was the shining yellow of daffodils, and his skin had a golden glow. A year round, built-in tan. How happy they were going to be!

'Look, we turn off here, where it says 'illage"

The name of the village had worn off the old sign some time ago.

'I'm glad you told me, Leo. You'd think it would signpost the town.'

'Well, it's a long way round to go to the town, whichever way you look at it.'

They had wound on through the moors, twilight turning to dusk, turning to darkness. Making Sarah think of a Biblical invocation: between the two evenings.

They had been between the two evenings, and now it was dark. The thought of their brief and joyful courtship came into her mind suddenly. She shivered again. 'It really is getting cold now, Leo.'

'Ah, but there it is. Disraeli Hall.'

Leo stopped the car and gestured, but at that moment the threatening rain arrived, with monsoon force. Sarah could vaguely see large gates and tall trees that swallowed up the headlights. There was no sign of any other houses, any other lights.

They drove on through the dimly seen gates, and along an unexpectedly narrow and winding drive, hemmed in by trees and shrubs. That was when Sarah first thought of Rebecca, and of herself as the new bride approaching Manderley.

'Leo, if these aren't rhododendrons,

18

then they ought to be.' She gestured at the vegetation pressing in on them, scraping at the sides of the car.

'What they ought to be is cut back.' Leo put his mobile down, having alerted the Keepers of the House to his presence. 'We need staff. Derek and Ava are OK. Well, Ava's marvellous. We couldn't do it without her. But we are going to need to get some real money in to do what we want with the Hall.'

Sarah had been going to ask more; for instance, the money they had got for her London flat, wasn't that going to achieve marvels? But at that moment they turned sharply round another corner and skidded on gravel.

At last there was a light. The rest of it was confusion, welcoming voices, exclamations about What a Downpour. Maggs taking the bags; watching her with his charming cat's smile. Ava ... Thinking back, Sarah could remember little about Ava Maggs except her intense thinness and cold calculator eyes above a welcoming smile.

Then, somehow, they were shivering in a large stone hall. It smelt of age. Old stone. Generations of old families. A wonderful smell, thought Sarah. So welcoming. Though it would have been even more welcoming to have found a log fire burning in the enormous fireplace that was just one of the details of the entrance hall.

Or to have found an old family waiting for them. Leo's family. The thought died in Sarah's mind as she began to take in her surroundings. She laughed, holding her hands out to the dusty dried flower display that was lost in the stony hearth. 'You could put my flat in there, light it, and still have room for the logs.' To her surprise, Leo gave her a *Pas Devant les Domestiques* look. Which made her want to giggle some more. It took her a while to realise that you never gave Ava an ounce more information than you had to, and a rather longer time to realise how much Leo traded on her information-gathering abilities.

'Annie's asleep,' Mrs M said. With a distinctly warning note to her voice.

'Annie. Yes. How is she, Ava? Poor little soul. She can meet her new mummy tomorrow. You don't mind keeping her with you for the next couple of nights, do you, Ava?'

'Of course not, Leo.'

That jarred a little, Sarah thought. But not because she'd been imagining servants who sirred and ma'amed them! How embarrassing that would have been.

What had she been expecting? It had all happened so quickly, she hardly knew. But not exactly this cold stone hall and this informal welcome. Where were Leo's family? That was followed by the thought: *who* were Leo's family?

The Cavaliers were a jumble of unrelated jigsaw pieces in her mind.

There was a famous old family. Going back to the time of the Cavaliers, she supposed. There was the well-known anecdote about Benjamin Disraeli and his numinous weekend stay at Cavalier Hall. There was the renaming of Hall and village street in honour of the great man. And a brief period of prosperity had followed. She knew that Leo was an orphan like herself. And, doubly orphaned, an only child. There were no siblings to help bear the loss, to share the memories.

And, above all, poor Leo, so golden and made for sunshine, was a widower. His young wife had been killed in a car crash.

It must have been on the road they had just driven down. She had never given it a thought. But it must have been. All those bends! Just add the ice, and the massive trunks of the old trees, clustering so closely round every bend in the road. Christmas, wasn't it? Sarah wondered where she'd been driving to on Christmas Eve, with the baby. Midnight mass, perhaps? Leo said she was a Catholic. Poor Leo. Poor girl. Poor baby Anya. Leo complained bitterly about the new road, but if only it had been there then ...

Sarah was relieved not to have to meet her little stepdaughter tonight. Everything was so strange. One minute they were at the Brompton Road Registry Office, showers of friends throwing biodegradable confetti all over them. My friends, thought Sarah. She wondered why Leo's friends hadn't come. Well, it was a long way for such a short wedding. Leo had told her how much he hated London.

'You come through here, Sarah, where there's a fire. You're shivering.' Derek Maggs proffered this most welcome invitation. 'This is the small drawing room.'

It was small compared to the hall, but

not small enough to be either cosy or warm. One bar of an old electric heater over in the corner had been turned on. Only just, and not often, to judge by the smell of burning dust. It had probably only gone on as Leo made his call from the driveway.

A hot drink would have been nice, but Ava bought over the whisky decanter and four glasses, which Leo was perfectly happy with, and they sat there till the bottle was finished. By the other three. Sarah wasn't drinking alcohol at the moment. Her tumbler remained full and untouched.

A feeling of blankness and unreality was coming over her, preventing her from noticing how carefully Ava Maggs was noting what she did not drink. Was she a threat, wasn't she? asked Ava's eyes, but Sarah barely registered it. It felt like a dream. Hardly surprising, she told herself. You get married for the first time at thirty-three, after a whirlwind courtship, and leave a high-powered city job and hard-won Islington flat to come up to the North of England.

'Do you know, Leo, I really never have been North of Watford before!'

But now Leo and Derek were deep in conversation, with Ava supervising intently. Sarah was able to study her for the first time. Ava wore tight blue denims, topped with a series of woolly tops. She obviously felt the cold all right. Her hair was very auburn, but Sarah was to find that this did not guarantee what colour it would be in the near future. It was immaculately styled, and her fingernails were professionally polished. She had the lined face of the heavy smoker and was obviously younger than she looked. At first glance, Sarah hadn't been able to work out whether Derek was her son or her husband. But she had held his hand possessively while introductions were made, so it seemed they were husband and wife.

She gazed at her new home. The roof was high, the mouldings lovely. The fireplace was of black marble, very tall and stately. How she longed for a roaring fire. Maybe that would be her first achievement: every room with a roaring fire. Warmth comes to Disraeli Hall again. Carpets would help too. And some curtains. She had begun to realise how bare the place was. The floor was parquet, fine in its time, but worn and damaged now. Rugs of indeterminate pattern were strewn about thinly, and there were no curtains at the windows. The blackness of the gardens stared in at them.

And the furniture ... They were sitting in unremarkable armchairs, worn and faded, the sort of thing you might have found outside any junk shop before fire safety laws more or less banished second-hand upholstered furniture. There was a cheap-looking sideboard, a ladder-back chair by the door that looked 'good', and a chipped, upholstered footstool lying forlornly in the corner. The heavy slate clock on the mantelpiece looked good too. It said 3.30, and had presumably being saying that for a long time.

Well, she wasn't in Manderley after all. That had been a country house in its prime, comfortable, warm, furnished with priceless antiques. She would have to think of another story. But she was tired, and yawning. She looked at her watch. Only 8.00! It felt like midnight. Whatever were they going to do with the rest of the evening?

What about unpacking? And Annie? Were they really not to see her tonight? She felt both excited and apprehensive about the prospect of instant motherhood. And hugged to herself the knowledge that she and Leo were already …

'I've put you both in the back.' Ava Maggs was blowing smoke in her direction and smiling charmingly. Her eyes didn't change, though. 'Derek and I are in the front at the moment. The roof is leaking so badly into the front bedrooms. You don't want to put up with all that. Not on your honeymoon. An old married couple like us, we don't mind where we are.'

You probably wouldn't mind knitting happily at the guillotine while my head dropped into the basket, Sarah found herself thinking. And I imagine you have a better bedroom than we do.

They smiled at each other, Sarah hoping that her eyes didn't give as much away as Ava's did.

CHAPTER 3

Sunlight poured in through the small window, which was frilled with shabby floral curtains. The sky showed in blue squares, a few white clouds puffing across. Sarah looked at cream walls, sloping and crooked. And old, blackened beams. I'm in Disraeli Hall, she thought, a sudden rush of energy propelling her feet into their slippers. Her new family home. The old family home. Brrr. It was a chilly place, though. Central heating, double glazing. That would be her first task. Thank goodness Summer was on the way.

Sarah reached for her dressing gown. It was a silk robe she had bought on their Thai trip. She would need something a bit warmer. She wrapped it round her, remembering the steamy heat of Bangkok, and walked to the window.

Perfect! A little cobbled courtyard, with fruit trees. Would she be looking out on pear blossom? Apple blossom? A lovely rounded stone wall.

Almost perfect. As just beyond the wall lay cranes and builders rubble. The business of the new road was already beginning to announce itself in subdued roars and whirrs.

She turned back and found Leo sound asleep. He looked at one with the sunshine, Sarah thought. They were such a contrast in the few wedding photos. She was so dark, Leo so fair. But her skin was pale, where his was golden. And good-looking! Too good-looking, she had thought when she first met him at that party, and had paid no attention to all his compliments and flirting.

How quickly he had shown her he was serious.

There was so much to do. So much to see. She wanted to tour the house and grounds. She couldn't wait to get started on making the Hall home. And what a lovely day it was turning out to be. A perfect Spring day.

She tiptoed about, dressing carefully, so as not to disturb Leo, who was obviously worn out from all the driving yesterday. The honeymoon must be over, thought Sarah. We both fell asleep as soon as our heads touched the pillow.

What a charming room it was, for all Ava's remarks about back bedrooms. It had narrow windows with deep sills, and oddly shaped walls, although it too was shabbily and shoddily furnished. The bed was small, old and saggy. The sheets were linen. Old, but spotless, and icy cold.

There was a small dressing table. Low, of good old wood, with a tall, tarnished mirror. A cupboard, its doors chipboarded for some odd reason, that opened to reveal a few old metal hangers, and one old children's hanger with an old-fashioned Jack Tar sailor's head on it. Had this room been the night nursery once?

So much to ask Leo. When he woke up.

There were two bedside tables, cheap and plywoody, with pretty old-fashioned china bedside lamps on them.

The wiring! Sarah checked the plugs. And that all seemed to have been done. Which was a relief. Wiring, Roofing, Damp proofing, all those sorts of things, were dreadfully discouraging. They took ages, cost a fortune, and made the house look worse while they were being done. Sarah remembered them only too well from her own flat. She had felt as if she was spending a lot of money going nowhere.

Well, if she was going to explore, she might as well get this room done thoroughly, she thought, and quietly checked the bedside cupboard on her side. The drawer was lined with floral paper. Not new. And there was a broken comb wedged at the back. In the little cupboard below was a beautiful Victorian chamber pot covered with lilacs.

Wherever Leo and Varya had slept, it wasn't here. This room hadn't been lived in for a long time.

Oddly, there was a door beside the fireplace. Sarah opened it cautiously and found it contained a steep and narrow flight of stairs, obviously going up to the attics. How strange. And exciting. She tiptoed up, expecting to find a long low attic crammed to the rafters with interesting, dusty old things, and was disappointed to find only a small square room with a grimy window, empty but for dust and a water tank. Where had everything gone to?

Longing to explore, but not wanting to wake the others sleeping in the house – presumably only the Maggses apart from her and Leo – she decided to try downstairs. Oh; and somewhere, little Anya was sleeping a calm and childish sleep, probably unaware of the change about to come into her life. There was darkness at the bottom of the back staircase, and she crashed about a bit in a hushed sort of way till she found the door to the low passage that led to the library and to some of the splendours she had been expecting.

Here were ceiling high shelves full of books, even a little – what would it be called? – a kind of mezzanine walkway with small tables and chairs. Enormous windows looked out on to mown lawns surrounded by a mosaic of rhododendrons and azaleas.

And a window seat!

Sarah tried it for size. Perfect. The shabby chintz cushions were comfortable, the garden view just as it should be. She could browse here for hours, learning all about the family.

That was going to be one of her jobs: to go through all the old documents in the library, and the family Bibles, and compile a more detailed genealogical record; a record for their children.

What a paradise for them to grow up in! Sarah hugged herself, thinking of her own childhood in her grandmother's tiny rented flat, surrounded by bleak streets of grey terraced houses, dwarfed by brutal towers of flats. And traffic.

Why hadn't they gone to the parks? To Kensington Gardens? Didn't children need green, and the earth? Her father had taken her to somewhere called the Woodland Gardens once. It had been a dream of paradise, alley upon alley of azaleas in splendid flower, with the saturated glowing colours of the Bangkok silks she and Leo had just bought rather a lot of. It was a long ride on the tube, and a long walk. Much too much for you, her mother had said, when asked why they couldn't go there themselves.

'We can't all afford cars,' she had added sharply.

Perhaps that was when a division had started to come between her and Jim. She had begun to envy him for staying with their father, for having car rides all the time, and then for having another brother when her father married 'that tart from the office'. She envied him for living in a big house with a garden.

Sarah's new stepmother simply refused to have her visit once she hit her teens. And, looking back, Sarah couldn't blame her. She felt increasingly bad for what she had put her own mother and gran through. Her gran was old and tired. And ill. And her mother was working, working, working all the time, sustained only by her various medications.

If only we didn't start life so selfish, if only we could go back and put it right.

You can't, Sarah, so it's no use thinking about it, she told herself firmly. Forget the past and all its mistakes. Make a wonderful life for our children here. A son. Leo must have a son. He himself only had the Hall because of the failure of the last Cavalier to produce a male heir, or indeed any heir at all. So, a son first, as Leo already has a daughter.

Then another son. A heir and a spare! How important that sounds. And then another daughter.

Four children, including Anya. That would be perfect! And a house this size needs many children to grow up in it, or it dies.

Well, she would meet Anya today. But she wasn't going to think about that too much. It would work or it wouldn't. She would simply have to do her best. Sarah found she was glad, though, that Anya was only three. Because, she told herself, any older and she wouldn't be happy about the kind of influence that Ava Maggs might have exerted.

But Mrs M was something else Sarah didn't want to think about.

Their honeymoon! She would think about that. Could there have been a more perfect two weeks? The island was so tiny you could walk right round it in ten minutes. The sea was clear and blue and turquoise and filled with fish so bright that you almost expected their paint to still be wet. At night, the air was full of the honey smell of frangipani. And the houseboy left its blossoms strewn on their bed every night.

'He doesn't know we are on our honeymoon does he?' Sarah had asked Leo, alarmed. He had laughed and told her that they did this for all the guests. He had been here before of course.

It was a perfect two weeks. The only two perfect weeks of my life. Two perfect weeks, to add to the one perfect day in Paradise with my father, when I wasn't so much older than Annie. Expensive though. It had taken a bite out of the money they got from selling Sarah's flat. Leo had wanted to go on – to stay longer in Thailand on the way back, even to travel on to Malaysia.

Shouldn't a gong be sounding to summon them to breakfast? Sarah was hungry. She looked at her watch: nine o'clock. On a Wednesday. Surely it wasn't too early to go and find something to eat. Who made breakfast for the household?

She hadn't quite expected there to be other people living in the house with them. Anyway, Derek Maggs looked like fun, and Ava would just have to be coped with.

She slid off the window seat and walked along by the library shelves, noticing for the first time that although the books were old, and some lovely and gilded, the shelves were far from full.

Perhaps the best had already been skimmed from this library and gone to wherever all the gorgeous old furniture that must have been here once had gone. There were still some pictures, though, some gloomy ancestors in oil, and a dark storm at sea. She had so much to discover, so much to find out, so much to do. Her life now seemed full of an importance and purpose she had despaired of ever finding.

Sarah set off to find the kitchens. She must have a cup of tea at least. And found herself puzzled. She tried every door off the main hall. There was an enormous, cold, unfurnished room on the side opposite the library. It had the same window seats and a view of gravel drive, flowers and woodland. The second door led into the room they were in last night. It still had four dirty glasses and an empty whisky bottle on the table, and the view through the windows at the back proved to be into a walled garden, neglected and overgrown. It could have been a herb garden, Sarah thought. How lovely if they could restore that.

OK, she told herself. The kitchens would obviously be down the large corridor by the imposing front staircase.

But all it led to was a door to the ruined garden, passing a large cloakroom en route.

Sarah stood by the cold, flower-filled fire in the big hall, puzzled. There was a smell of coffee from somewhere. She followed the coffee smell back into the library, and to the door at the back that led to the corridor she had already come from. It was a low cosy corridor, quiet in its cream and black, obviously part of the original farmhouse that had been the beginnings of Disraeli Hall some centuries ago. It led her back to the dark at the bottom of the second staircase, where Sarah found a door she hadn't noticed earlier.

It led straight to the kitchens.

'You're an early bird.'

That was Ava Maggs, surprised. Dressed in tight blue jeans, woolly slippers and several woollen jumpers, she was heating up cups of coffee in the microwave. The kitchen was long and

41

old-fashioned. Not somewhere you could sit.

Sarah followed Ava through to a sunny breakfast room. Derek sat one end of a large wooden table, reading The Mirror. The window behind him gave a vista of roads and cranes and cones.

'That's what woke you up, the Tramway,' he said. 'This is the last section; the rest is finished. Trams won't come up here, though.'

'That must've upset Leo.'

'Leo and I had a long talk about it. And I got him calmed down. It'll be useful for us, this road, and it doesn't spoil the front.' Ava spoke possessively of Leo, obviously not prepared to allow that he could have an emotion she had not already accounted for and monitored.

I must have been quite a shock to you, then, thought Sarah with some satisfaction, as she asked about tea bags.

'I'm afraid we're coffee drinkers here. I'm not sure there's a tea bag in the house.'

Derek winked at her. 'We've got tea bags somewhere in the cupboards. I'll do you one. You can't make tea in the microwave so it's not on Ava's menu.'

Mrs M lit another cigarette from the stump of the old one. 'I've more than enough to do as it is, without cooking.'

Sarah wondered what exactly it was she did do. Not cook. And certainly not dust, or light fires. Maggs obviously cared for the garden, in that the lawns were mown, and the drive at the imposing frontage and turning circle was weed free with neat flower beds.

'Where's Anya? Has she had her breakfast yet?' Sarah was apprehensive about her new stepdaughter and wanted to get the first awkward meeting over with.

Derek looked at Ava quizzically. 'Oh,' Ava waved a cigarette towards the kitchens, 'Debbie'll bring her when she comes.'

'Debbie?'

'Yes, Debbie, she helps me out. Goodness knows how we get through it with just the two of us and Debbie's mum, but we do. Annie spent the night with them. They never mind having her.'

Poor Annie. She seemed to be farmed out to anyone who would have her. It was time Leo and I got here, thought Sarah. I don't like the sound of any of this.

'Yes, well, she'll be here with us from now on. Which is her bedroom?'

Sarah had left her upstairs exploration unfinished. She didn't want to open a door and find Ava and Derek tucked up in a four-poster. She had risked a short search and found a large, cold and old-fashioned bathroom, and had a sketchy sort of lukewarm shower. That was something else that must be seen to quickly. There was no reason not to have at least one warm bathroom and constant hot water.

'Oh, we'll have to fix her something up. She's been down with the Brats most of the time; and Professor Plant took her the week they were away. Canvassing.'

What had been going on here? Whatever all that meant, it seemed clear that all during their courtship, perhaps ever since her mother's death, poor Annie had been pushed around like an unwanted parcel.

'Yes, I will check out the bedrooms today and decide where she is going to go.' And go out and buy some furniture if necessary. She could see that Ava didn't like it, but Derek was amused.

'Don't worry, Sarah, Annie loves being at the Brats; the twins are her age. And she's been there most of the time. It's just that Flutterby's been away to London for the selection committee, so

Annie has been staying with the Plants until last night.'

Nothing in that sentence made any sense to Sarah, but she realised that Derek was telling her it was OK. He saw she was worried and he understood.

There was the sound of a door somewhere in the back kitchen, a 'Hiya,' and Debbie arrived. Alone.

'Where's Anya?' Sarah said it rather sharply; realizing only later that she had played right into Ava's hands by alienating Debbie, who wouldn't be spoken to 'like that'.

Debbie gave her a look. 'Annie's stayed at the Plant's. Me mum went for her last night but she said she wanted to stay there.'

'Oh, yes, I'm afraid I don't know any of these people yet.' Or these awful children, the brats, Sarah thought. 'Debbie, hello, I'm Sarah, Leo's wife.'

Debbie looked at Sarah's outstretched

hand and took it limply, in a way that made Sarah feel foolish.

She was a pretty dark-haired girl. Small, and with a very flirtatious manner. She paid no further attention to Sarah, but sat down for a coffee with Derek, and they began to banter together in what was obviously their usual way.

How difficult it all is, thought Sarah. It must have been easier in the old days in some ways. The new mistress might have had a houseful of servants to deal with, but at least everyone knew what the rules were. What are the rules here? How should we all behave to each other?

Although face the facts, Sarah, she thought ruefully, if you had been here in the heyday of the Hall, you would have been under-scullery maid. She smiled into her tea as Leo suddenly bounded into the room, bringing his usual sunshine with him.

'So here you all are, nice and cosy.

Debbie!' He picked her up and whirled her.

She fluttered at him, with mock indignation. 'I'm not a little girl any more, Mr Cavalier. Just you put me down.'

'You shouldn't be so tiny, then. I can't resist you.'

Leo plonked himself down next to her, accepting the cup of coffee Mrs M held out. 'Where's your mum? Not late, the first morning I'm back? And Ava, what happened to my hot water this morning?'

'She's on her way, Mr Cavalier.' Debbie giggled. And, 'He's such a slave driver,' she appealed to Derek.

Sarah watched them all, feeling on the outside again. Leo's like a sultan with his harem. She sat and drank her tea as she watched Debbie flirting and teasing the two men under Mrs M's watchful eye. He's barely said good morning to me. His wife. Sarah looked for hurt feelings, for loneliness, exclusion, jealousy. And could find none.

She had known Leo three months, she thought. Three months of a wonderful courtship and two weeks of perfect honeymoon. And she must be very sure of him, because sitting here watching him, she suddenly knew for sure that he could flirt with Debbie till his head fell off and she wouldn't need to feel one pang of exclusion, let alone jealousy.

She probed at her feelings. That was good, surely? That was married life. So different from courtship. All the tumultuous feeling, all that uncertainty. No one could live with it for too long. It was wonderful not to be so young any more, to have made the right marriage, to have put all those uncertainties away forever.

Yet she couldn't account for the mixed emotions inside her. She had a feeling of coldness and alienation, a feeling of not belonging somehow. And she was troubled by a strange irritation that Debbie was monopolizing Derek Maggs. But above all, she felt the pull of truly strong emotion. Because, cold and half empty though it was, she loved Disraeli Hall.

CHAPTER 4

Sarah loved Anya, too, as it turned out.

Debbie's mother arrived empty-handed. She was simply an older version of her daughter. Which suggested that Debbie would be fine once she had outgrown her teenage haughtiness. And behind her a tall, soldierly gentleman trotted in with a tiny little blonde riding on his shoulders, holding on to his white hair and urging him to gallop faster.

He waited for a proper introduction to Sarah, kissed her hand in a courtly manner, then greeted everyone else with perfect old-fashioned politeness. He joined them in a coffee while Annie had some milk. She had breakfasted, he assured Sarah. He and Ophelia always breakfasted at 7.30 sharp, he informed them gravely. But not judgmentally.

She liked Professor Plant. And he seemed to like her. His English was still slightly halting, even after all these years exiled from his Eastern European homeland, yet somehow he fitted the Hall with his old-fashioned manners, his stateliness, the touch of formality he brought to the atmosphere. Because the Hall wasn't really a place for lounging about in blue jeans, over microwaved coffee; some formality was necessary, surely. And she and Leo had wonderful plans for restoring it. It was such a mini-stately home that it could be a family home once again. It wasn't impossible. Her money would fix the roof. And together they were going to take on the Peak Park authorities and see if they could wrest permission from them for a couple of holiday cottages, created from outbuildings that were placed discreetly in the remote gardens.

Her strange, cold feelings had vanished with the arrival of Anya. She would come to feel at home here, she really would. For she already loved the

Hall and its golden squire, Leo, and the wonderful children they would have. If the love of courtship was turning into married love, nothing could be better. And she loved that little Alice in Wonderland girl, Anya.

She was a solemn, blonde child with a sudden enchanting smile. Her sturdy little body matched her personality. She seemed equal to her situation. Father and daughter met up without much enthusiasm. Never mind, poor Annie would be forgiven for not being a boy once their own son had arrived safely.

'I'm going to fix her up a bedroom today, Leo.'

'Sure.'

Sarah was interested to see what would happen next; what Debbie herself and Ava and Derek would be doing. What was the routine here?

She realised that she longed to talk to Leo about it. When were they going to be alone together?

'Another coffee, Leo? Professor Plant? There's some left in the pot. And what about you, Annie? Some milk?' Sarah felt it was now time to establish herself, and take a little control. For a start she wanted to see what Ava would do.

'Oh no, I'll get those. You sit down, Sarah.' Yes, that was predictable.

'Ava's the microwave supremo around here, and don't you forget it.' That was Derek. 'Do you want another tea?'

'Thanks.' Sarah longed to get on. There was so much to do, so much to explore. The whole of Disraeli Hall and its grounds lay before her. They would sort out Anya's bedroom and almost certainly buy some furniture for it. It was going to be such fun.

And then there were the gardens. It was a lovely day, too, and she had seen so little of them yet, just dark and windswept shrubs rattling against their car last night on that journey down the long narrow drive.

She must ask Leo about the front drive. Why not re-open it? It would make a much more imposing approach to the house. There was such scope here.

'Do we have a maze, or a secret garden, or anything?'

They all looked at her, surprised. 'No. 'Fraid not.' That was Leo. 'Not even a Priest's Hole. The Cavaliers always took care not to clash with the powers that be.'

'You mean you weren't Cavaliers?' Sarah was amazed.

'Not while Oliver Cromwell reigned supreme.' That was Professor Plant.

Ava rustled the coffee at them. 'Come along now, Debbie needs to get the kitchen cleared.' The conversation wasn't one that engaged her.

Derek handed Sarah a tea, and, having cleared the rest of the table, she sat down deliberately with it. 'We could have one, though.'

'What?'

'A maze. Or a secret garden. Or both.'

'Oh, give us time to get the roof done!' Leo groaned.

'Well, I see you have a busy time ahead of you. Any time you need a home for Anya, Ophelia and I will be delighted. We don't see nearly enough of our own grandchildren.' Professor Plant said his formal goodbyes.

Ava and her helpers were busy putting a load of washing in the machine, which was a large industrial strength one. Sarah rather hoped it might be something to do with curtains. Leo and Derek were helping themselves to a third cup of coffee. Derek had put the percolator on, she noticed. Now Sarah wished Derek would go as she wanted to be able to plan the day out with Leo. And to point out that if there was any chance of a maze, the sooner it was planted the better.

And her head was buzzing with plans

for the little ruined kitchen garden she had spotted. Well, 'small', she thought happily to herself, it was as big as two suburban gardens put together. And it was just a tiny part of their land. Their estate!

But somehow, planning eluded her. Ava managed to separate Leo and corral him and Derek into the garages for some discussion about cars, just as Anya required another trip to the large cloakroom that held the porcelain toilet engraved with blue blossoms. She was frightened of the dark under the second staircase and wouldn't go on her own. And then Sarah decided they would go upstairs and look at her bedroom and see what was wanted.

That turned out to be quite a lot because, apparently, Anya had been sleeping in the room she and Leo now occupied. All her belongings – not many – were in a large suitcase under the bed that seemed to have been kept permanently packed for her continual removals. She had barely a toy to her name.

There was a lot to do here. And how difficult for a tiny child to sleep on her own in this vast empty hall! OK, the Maggses were around, but somewhere 'in the front'.

'Show me where your Auntie Ava and Uncle Derek sleep, Annie.'

Annie put out her hand and took Sarah's confidently and led her off down a corridor past the servants' staircase to another door. They pushed through and found themselves on an imposing landing. The magnificent main staircase swept up here to four handsome carved doors.

Annie led them straight to the door on the left, which opened into a room of very pleasant proportions with enormous stone windows looking out over the front drive to the woodland and the moors beyond. There was a fancy king-size bed with zingy electric blue and black sheets and duvet set. The curtains were new and expensive, but chintzy, a modern chintz, with deep red poppies and blue cornflowers. There was something almost Chinese about the colours. And there was a thick black wool carpet. Sarah patted it, puzzled. Wool, very expensive. Black. Had it been made especially for the bedroom?

Well, this was where Leo and Varya had slept. Almost certainly. And now it had been colonized by the Maggses. How had that happened? Well, they could just un-colonise it.

Was she brave enough to put them into the back bedrooms, wondered Sarah. Probably not. But there were plenty of bedrooms in the front of Disraeli Hall.

She tried to visualize a Manderley style scene, Ava bursting in to find Sarah exploring her dead mistress's bedroom, which she'd kept exactly as it had been the day she died. Was there a balcony here which Mrs Ava Danvers could pressure her to jump off?

There wasn't any fog, though, which was the correct weather backdrop for the scene. Perhaps a haze of cigarette smoke would do?

Anyway, wouldn't Ava just shove her off the moment she wanted to? No, thought Sarah, she wouldn't. She would persuade someone else to do it, so cleverly that they would feel it was a moral crusade and think they had dreamt it up themselves. She shivered, cold again in the splendid frontage of the Hall. Why had she been so certain from the moment she looked into Ava's eyes?

'Let's explore, Annie, because I've never been here before.'

Annie was rather big-eyed about the whole enterprise but didn't seem to mind, and kept a trusting hold on Sarah's hand. Poor little soul. Who does she have, really? Sarah thought that, of all of them, she would most want to be with Derek or with Professor Plant and his wife.

She must meet Ophelia Plant, and these Brats, whoever they were. It seemed they'd all been good to Annie. And, the thought came to her, surprising her, she needed some allies around here, too.

But Leo was to be my best friend and ally, wasn't he? That moment of coldness and disconnection she had felt at breakfast, almost as if Leo, her husband, was a complete stranger; that was just tiredness and strangeness. Surely?

You slept fine though, Sarah, said a voice in her head, a new voice that she didn't want there. And when have you minded strangeness and new things?

But by the time they had finished their upstairs exploring and come back down by the imposing front staircase,

Sarah's head was awhirl with rooms and plans, all unwanted voices and strange cold feelings forgotten. What a shame she was descending those stairs for the first time in blue jeans and a jumper. She should at least have had on a morning gown. And perhaps be getting ready to accept callers; or to send Mrs M to tell them she wasn't at home.

'Right, now, Annie, don't tell me, I have to remember how to find this kitchen. Through the library, isn't it? I think we can do something about that without annoying the Peak Park Planners too much.'

The two halves of the house were somewhat awkwardly joined up when you started to use them, and there was that large pool of permanent darkness at the bottom of the second staircase. She was beginning to see the layout of the Hall clearly in her mind now, and if she let it simmer in her subconscious for a while, then a plan to join the old and the new better, the formal and the informal, would be sure to come.

Once safely past the darkness, they found the kitchens empty. The washing machine worked away in the scullery and a dishwasher splashed in the main kitchen. They weren't short of modern gadgets here, at any rate. Still hand in hand, they retraced their steps and found a sullen Debbie scrubbing out the downstairs cloakroom.

'Debbie. Do you know where Leo, Mr Cavalier, has got to?'

'I'm sure I don't know.' Debbie looked sullen; she obviously did know.

'Your mum, then, or Mrs Maggs?'

'They've gone down for the eggs,' Debbie said, with theatrical impatience. 'I've to do this floor now, IF you wouldn't mind.'

Please do, thought Sarah. And what eggs? Dinosaur eggs, if it took two of them to carry them back.

'There's too much to do to waste time,

Annie.' She snatched Annie's little red coat off the peg just before Debbie's mop got to that patch of floor. 'We'll go into town together, you and me. Tell Leo when he re-appears. Oh, and what about lunch? Am I expected back?'

Debbie sighed in an impatient but satisfied way and made no answer. Oh, the joys of adolescence. Please don't turn out like this, Annie, Sarah silently implored her step-daughter. If Debbie didn't bother to tell Leo where they had gone, so what? He hadn't bothered to tell her where he was going.

* * *

Sarah met Alan Brat, or rather Aleyn of Bratislav, his ancestor, in the library that afternoon as she was turning out a box of documents.

She and Annie had had a wonderful morning. Curtains had been bought, paint chosen. Annie now had toys and a toy chest. Sarah had felt a bit dashed to return to an empty hall, but she had made the most of her time. The little bedroom beside theirs was made up with a flower fairy coverlet and matching rug. The chest of drawers had its first coat of pink paint. And the curtains were waiting for Derek to fix the fittings.

The other little bedroom would be for their son. Their sons! And the room she and Leo were presently sleeping in would become the playroom. Or day nursery.

Sarah thought back to the rented accommodations of her own childhood and hugged herself. All those years she and her mother had slept on the old settee in her gran's scullery kitchen.

At lunchtime she had found Mrs M in the kitchen unwrapping a single portion chicken dish and inserting it into the microwave. Leo and Derek, she informed Sarah, were lunching at the Coat.

'The Coat?'

'The pub. Down by the Gatehouse.'

The village pub, presumably. Well, she and Annie wouldn't have minded joining them. It would have been better than sitting around with Ava Maggs sharing a tepid chicken dinner for one, and discussing ... what on earth would they discuss? No doubt there could be many cosy chats about the faults and failings of Dawn and Debbie. And then astoundingly intimate revelations about poor Derek, for which she would expect to be paid for in kind by equal indiscretions about Leo.

Sarah doubted that the concept of loyal love was something that Ava would have anything to do with. And she also presumed that the ladies had had a thrilling morning dissecting her. Would there be any chance of discussing anything other than personalities? Or diets? The history of the Cavaliers, perhaps? Or what had happened to the fine old furnishing that must at one time have filled the Hall?

Or they could contemplate the century that was just ending. After all, millenniums didn't loom every day of the week. Probably, for Ava, the twentieth century had been a wild success, notable for the invention of the frozen low-cal dinner and the microwave. If it had only succeeded in exterminating the calorie it would have been perfect. Sarah wondered why Maggs wasn't as whip-thin as his wife. How did he stay so sleek and solid? Perhaps, like a cat, he was fed elsewhere?

For some reason, the thought made her uneasy. And she bustled around boiling the eggs, which had been collected, as promised, and making toast for her and Annie, while Ava watched disapprovingly without offering to help. Sarah loaded everything on to a tray.

'Come on, Annie, we'll eat in the

library today.' She was not prepared to spend her whole life with Ava. Not even with Derek. So she might as well start as she meant to go on.

After she had returned the tray to the kitchen quarters, which were empty once again, and settled Annie down in the window seat for a nap with her new fluffy panda, she began to examine the contents of the library. Leo had spoken of a need to get all the family documents properly sorted and archived.

And he was right. They were all over the place. Never one to put off till tomorrow, Sarah began to collect them in piles on to the desk, trying to sort roughly as she went along. And in no time she found herself face to face with Aleyne of Bratislav.

Intriguingly, he had returned from some fearful crusade or other with the incumbent Cavalier and had made his home at the gates of the castle that had once stood there. And now here was this Alan Brat, a direct descendant, once again living at the gates of a Cavalier castle. And she felt she had to go down and see it. History alive! That's what she would plan for tomorrow, if it was OK with Leo.

CHAPTER 5

'Come on Annie, get your shoes on, we're going to go for a walk.'

'She hasn't had her breakfast yet,' Ava bustled in.

'Oh yes she has. A nice fresh egg and toast fingers.'

Ava picked up the special diet cereal discontentedly. 'That's good. My word, you will get to be a big girl, won't you, now you've got your new mummy? Come and give your Auntie Ava a goodbye kiss. And your Uncle Derek. You mustn't neglect us now you've got a new mummy.'

The words 'new mummy' were obviously going to be Ava's leitmotif for the day.

What a sensible little girl Annie was. Considering she was only three. She patiently trotted over and suffered a spikey Mrs M kiss, and allowed herself to be picked up and hugged by Derek. Actually, Derek's charm probably worked on women of all ages. He genuinely likes us, he really does, Sarah thought.

She was beginning to feel that Leo hadn't been much of a father to Anya. But then, she hadn't been a son, poor little soul, and he wanted a son so much. Needed one. And then there was the shock of her mother's death and he had to go a'wooing again. And met Sarah.

He'd been busy. And all the worries of restoring the Hall fell on him, too. She shouldn't really blame him for having got so smashed at the Coat yesterday. He needed a bit of relaxation before they got down to things. Perhaps Derek had been something of a father figure to Annie. If so, she was glad he was going to stay around. After all, Sarah and Leo could give her precious little in the way of uncles. Sarah's brother's was in Canada with his family, as far as she knew; they no longer even did Christmas cards. And Leo had no one.

'What about Varya's family?' Sarah was surprised to hear the words from inside her head come out of her mouth. But still, she did want to know. And at least Leo wasn't here. He never mentioned her name, or wanted it mentioned.

At last, Sarah had introduced a worthwhile topic of conversation, and Ava Maggs hissed sideways through enjoyably pursed lips that, yes, Varya, did have a cousin, second-cousin or something, he said he was. It was the sort of 'said' that was usually followed by: 'but if you ask me'. And sure enough, if you asked Ava, (whether you asked her or not), she was of the opinion that he was simply sniffing round to see if there was money now Varya had married the local squire, and was of very questionable cousinhood.

'Looked nothing like her for a start.

Nothing. He was as fair as Leo. Varya was dark, like you.'

'Oh, come on Ava, Stephan was all right. I don't think he was a cousin, though. I think he was the ex-boyfriend. And still mad about her if you ask me. She was a gorgeous girl. He likes them pretty, does Leo.'

Derek was looking at her with a frank appreciation that Sarah ought perhaps to have found sexist but somehow found reassuring.

'Uncle Step, Uncle Step.' That was Annie, enthusiastically joining in the conversation.

'See, she hasn't forgotten him!' Derek looked down at her fondly. 'Come on sweetheart, I'll give you and your new mummy a ride down to the Crescent.' Had he put the words 'new mummy' in inverted commas, Sarah wondered?

Before she could protest, not that she especially wanted to, Sarah found that she and Annie were in Derek's Land

Rover heading off down a finished bit of the brand new Tramway towards the abode of the mysterious Aleyne of Bratislav.

'The bungalow belonged to Alan's parents. They built it after they got married, but when they retired they decided to move down to the South Coast to be near her sister, so Alan and Flutter bought it off them. Bognor Regis I think it is they went to. Nice down there, plenty of sunshine.'

Maybe, thought Sarah, but this isn't exactly what I was hoping for. She had wanted something romantic. Not bungalows and Bognor Regis.

'It's only a short walk through the grounds, but it's right muddy today.' Derek turned off into a side road and suddenly, there were the grey stone town walls in front of them. They turned left into Disraeli Crescent and left again into a small unadopted cobbled road, Disraeli Close. And there was the bungalow. Neat, modern, red brick, with a garden in which the lawn had been ironed and every leaf polished and pressed.

Next to it was an old cottage, as untidy and overgrown as the bungalow was neat, and beyond it the Gatehouse for Disraeli Hall. Long deserted, it was of the inevitable grey stone, gaunt and empty. The row of terraced stone cottages was obviously tenanted. It was clear they were lived in by people who had no skills in putting things in the dustbins, or putting out the dustbins for collection.

And opposite the houses was a shabby old pub, the scene of yesterday's debauchery. They had rolled home at after midnight, Derek and Leo. Singing. At least, Leo had been although she had got nothing but groans from him this morning. Derek, on the other hand, was as sleek and glossy as ever. Perhaps he had just had a saucer of cream or something.

'I didn't know the old Cavaliers renamed the village streets too.'

'Oh yes. They even thought about calling The Coat the Disraeli Arms.' Derek waved towards the old pub, where Joseph and his Coat of Many Colours creaked gently on a faded signboard.

'Oh, yes, neat. I'm glad they didn't change it.' It made up a bit for the bungalowed Aleyne. 'Anyway, its Biblical, isn't it?' She remembered Joseph and his brothers and his coat from a book of Bible stories her gran used to read to her.

Derek looked blank. 'I mean he was Jewish, wasn't he, Disraeli? So a Biblical name for the pub seems right.' Sarah explained.

'Want a half?' Derek dealt with all such flights of fancy swiftly.

'Oh. No. We can't do that. To be honest, I came to look at Aleyne of Bratislav and his wife. Or wyve, I suppose it would be.'

'You'll be disappointed. And Flutterby's a very modern woman too. Come on, Annie, you'd like a milkshake, wouldn't you?'

But Anya was already heading up Aleyne's neat front path, saying something that sounded like, 'Wills and Harry'.

* * *

Either Bratislavans were very much like Yorkshiremen, or the Brat line had been swamped by Yorkshireness in the intervening centuries, because Alan was every inch a Yorkshireman; solid, stolid, handsome; blonde, with blue eyes. He kept his feet firmly planted on the ground.

'Willoughby! Harrington!' he called authoritatively, and two little boys of about Annie's age toddled down the path. They were solemn children, as Anya was, and they greeted each other seriously and began to chase each other slowly round the immaculate lawn.

'Keep to the path! I'll not have that grass walked on, as you well know. And shoes off before you come in the house!' Alan was an old-fashioned kind of dad.

Sarah thought they made a charming scene, though. The boys, obviously twins, were very like their father, but darker and with brown eyes. The exotically named Flutterby seemed to have brought something other than Yorkshire and Bratislava to the mix. Sarah couldn't wait to meet her.

The bungalow was as immaculate as the garden. Impossible to imagine that two young boys lived here! The children had left their shoes outside the front door, as ordered, and sat in a circle round a 'nice, quiet' game of coloured building bricks, Alan shushing them sternly when they got a little excited. Sarah wondered if she and Derek should take their shoes off, but as they hadn't committed the crime of running on the lawn, they would probably get away with it.

'Would you like a cup of tea? Flutter'll be back in a moment, she's with the Daughters. They are laying the plans for some coup at the AGM.' Making tea, entertaining, was obviously women's work. Aleyne of Bratislav, having now done his myne host bit, began to talk to Derek about the Tramway, in which he took a keen interest. He seemed capable of speculating endlessly on all the different route possibilities the Tramway would provide.

Whose daughters? Sarah wondered. It seemed clear that Alan and Flutterby just had the two sons. And what AGM?

And where are these eggs coming from? Sarah had noticed a basket of brown eggs in the immaculate Brat kitchen. They seemed a little out of place as they still had bits of straw on them. They were not the glamorized eggs of the supermarket but the same as the ones at the hall. Really fresh ones, and really free-range too. From hens that ran and scratched and pecked things up, and whose supplements were household scraps, not fishmeal pellets, so that the eggs came out tasting of the sea. Could it be that Disraeli Hall actually had a Home Farm?

So much to do! So much to find out! She was really enjoying it all, and just wished that Leo was there to share it with her, instead of lying in a darkened room in Disraeli Hall groaning over aspirins and black coffee.

No Flutterby appeared and, after a while, they decided to adjourn to The Coat. Apparently the politics of the AGM were proving more tedious then usual. Mrs Aleyne of Bratislav sounded like the sort of person who would be active in the WI, perhaps on the Jam-Making Quango or something.

The Coat of Many Colours was dark.

Cosy, old, and unreconstructed, it felt as comfortable as an old shoe. No wonder Leo spent all yesterday here. He was probably feeling as strange as she was. After all, thought Sarah, who knows how he really feels about Varya's death. She certainly didn't, and she wasn't sure that she wanted to. They had to go on from where they were now. They hardly knew each other yet, if she was honest with herself. It was all going to take time, and she didn't need a Rebecca-like obsession with her predecessor. There was simply no point. Their new life started now. Especially when ... she patted her tummy softly.

Professor Plant was standing by the pool table, playing a rather wobbly game of pool neither his eyesight nor his legs being what they had been in the heyday of Disraeli Crescent. Sarah felt even more at home to think she already knew at least one of the regulars at what was certainly going to be their Local.

The Coat was quiet, apart from the chatter, the click of the pool balls, the thud of darts and the clash of glasses. Which is to say there was no jukebox, no canned music, no karaoke. And there, glowing out of a dark corner as she held court, was Flutterby Brat.

It turned out that the local chapter of The Daughters of the Windrush met there every first Saturday of the month, and the meeting was just ending, so Sarah was able to talk to a few of the departing Daughters. It seemed that you were eligible if your grandparents had come over on the Windrush. They seemed to consider themselves the only true Brits and took a patronising but kindly attitude towards all those who had arrived later.

From their account of their gallant leader, Flutterby seemed to be shooting up the path her Windrush ancestors had set before her. She, who could have been a supermodel, was heading straight for Parliament. There was a safe Lib-Dem seat going in the Peak Park and Flutterby hoped to be up for it. The incumbent, Freddy Ramsbottom, who had been there forever, was even now awaiting further heart surgery and certainly could not go on being there forever. The Selection Committee was on standby. They had never had a woman selected before. But Fred was a Lancashire lad, so they were used to strangeness.

Pity in a way that it wasn't a Conservative seat coming vacant, because then she would be sure to get selected. No Conservative selection committee would ever be able to resist that hat, Sarah mused, while Flutterby held the table entranced with her views on the necessity of making sure that all young people worked for a living.

The hat was the clear orange of the inside of a daffodil flower, and it perched on the side of her dark curls in a quite magical way. Her jacket, very expensive – Armani possibly? – a soft wool, matched it exactly. The dress underneath was of silk, and of a green as clear and springlike as the orange.

Her skin was the colour that blondes who want to be on holiday brochures have to tan to. And her eyes were enormous, like Bambi's. Hypnotic. Fringed with lashes so long and curly that they surely couldn't be real. The lashes were a puzzle Sarah didn't solve. But she never saw Flutterby without them.

She really was quite a bore with her politics, Sarah thought after a while. Not that any man was ever going to notice that. And anyway, it was pleasant and soothing to sit there and feel so accepted. No one in The Coat seemed to see her in any way as an unlikely choice for Leo's wife, a surprising choice, a worse choice than Varya, a better choice than Varya. She was just Leo's wife, and they simply made room for her round the table. It was restful. It was part of what she married Leo for, thought Sarah, a sudden feeling of joy and Springtimeiness coming over her. Call it a rooted life, a community, acceptance, stability; she couldn't exactly put a name to it. Because she had never had it. There had just been a few brief glimpses like that day in Paradise with her father. But she suddenly felt it here with these people.

CHAPTER 6

Before her first month at Disraeli Hall was over, Sarah had worked out that there would be no new roof. Not for a while. The money from her flat appeared to be pretty much all the money there was. And that would be needed to pay staff wages and basic living costs. And it wasn't going to last very long, either.

Leo's 'occupation', as something in antiques, seemed to have been confined to selling off the Hall's fine furniture as fast as he could. He had been down selling the last decent pictures when she had met him at the party. They still had a fair chunk of that money in the bank, as Sarah had managed to stop Leo extending the honeymoon into a round the world tour.

But from what she had gleaned from Derek and the Plants, it was Varya who had done the real professional dealing and had got some decent prices. It was she who had contacted the London auction houses and dealerships. The local buyers had not been pleased by her arrival as they had been doing so well out of Leo.

And it was she who had got a lot of the unglamorous and basic work on the Hall done. Damp courses had been put in, walls had been replastered, the whole place had been rewired. Whereas Leo had wanted a cruise and an indoor pool.

Sarah was beginning to discover a fellow feeling for her predecessor.

So Derek and Ava stayed in possession of their film star bedroom. The little they were paid warranted perks. And it also meant that Ava was able to spend half the week working at the Riding Stables in what had once been the Home Farm without anything being said. She was a great horsewoman, control being her thing.

The eggs didn't come from the farm, though. They were produced by Professor Plant's chickens, and Sarah had quickly taken over all egg collecting duties for herself. She also took down the bags of weeds and clippings, and later on windfall pears, that helped to feed the Plant menagerie. Their hens were free range – and they kept rabbits too. The professor had been a country child and often talked of the tiny farm, forever lost to him, along with most of his family, after Stalin and his cohorts arrived.

She found she needed her time spent on Disraeli Crescent with the Plants. Their large stone house seemed more like home than the Hall had yet managed to do. And she felt reassured by Ophelia, who had sailed successfully through all her pregnancies and also coped with innumerable grandchildren. She had even begun to feel that the tiny lost Chateau Plant had been her childhood home, too. She wondered why her parents had never talked about the past, any more than her gran had. It was as if they had been lost in time, stranded in the present with no clear idea how they got there, or how to escape.

'Come on, Annie, we'll go over and see your Auntie Plant. We'll get the eggs and see what she's having for lunch.'

Sarah was hoping for an invitation. She wanted to talk to the Plants about the Hall, but also she was fascinated by their tales of Disraeli Crescent in its heyday. And anyway, she and Annie had eaten too many solitary lunches in the library. Leo was off at the stables with Ava. Something about hunters. Were they actually hunting, in fact? Was this the hunting season? Didn't that start on the 14th of July or something? He had been out doing his country squire pursuits ever since they arrived, while Sarah struggled with the Hall. And, understandably, he didn't want her near a horse until afterwards.

She had decorated their bedroom in creams and blacks. She had found some lovely old Victorian fireplace tiles with poppies and blue cornflowers in one of the cellars, and had got Derek to lay them round the little fireplace. She had discovered the weekly town markets and found cheap and cheerful chintzy material and made some curtains. She had decided that as long as the Maggses occupied the front bedroom, she and Leo would stay in the back. They would at least be guaranteed some privacy that way.

She had taken over the shopping, and all the basics came from the market now, thus halving the household bills. She had also made giant steps with the Cavalier paperwork, and imported several large filing cabinets, which Leo grumbled about. She had made a decision that the Gatehouse would be restored, whatever it cost. She had quietly had a surveyor in and he had confirmed that structurally it was fine. Derek and Ava could live there, rent free. That would be their perk. And, in time, when she and Leo could manage without the Maggses – and she was determined that time would come – they would probably sell it and use the money to further their ambitions for the Hall.

Then she and Leo would reclaim the front of the house, and get the roof done. Assuming that there really was a problem with the front roof. For all the Spring rain, Sarah had seen no sign of an inflow yet. And by that time, the bedrooms and nursery would be ready for the children.

Children, she thought, hugging herself. She was going to be the mother of children. At last.

And, above all, she had looked after Anya. Which appeared to be a full time job. Ophelia and Flutterby had laughed when she blurted that one out, and said just to wait till she and Leo had their baby.

But so far she had loved her new role. She had worked out a little routine for them. They met for breakfast at 7.30, before the others were about. Sarah laid the table for them both and cleared it before Ava and Derek got anywhere near the kitchen. She had found a set of pretty cream cereal bowls with dark green pine cones round the rim. Each one had a different animal in the bottom.

The first game of the day was to set Annie's cereal out with some seasonal fresh fruit chopped in, and she had to guess whether she had Bertie Badger, Ferdy Fox, or Harry Horse. That ensured a cereal bowl scraped clean. They spent the morning playing doing things round the house. If Sarah was painting furniture, Annie could be settled next to her with paints and a big sheet of paper. There were so few carpets in the Hall it was wonderfully easy to find space for these things.

Sarah wondered how different her own childhood would have been if the three of them had just had a bit of space. There had barely been room enough for her gran in that tiny basement flat. And yet she had moved over, for all those years, and shared with her suddenly husbandless daughter and fatherless granddaughter ... sadness was not good now. Sarah stopped that chain of thought firmly. She must think happy positive thoughts for the sake of the baby that was coming.

They had lunched together nearly every day in the library, she and Anya, off a tray, in the big window seat. Often they had a Plant egg, or perhaps beans on toast, or maybe soup Sarah had made.

She longed for the day that she could

be out and about in her own kitchen garden, picking salad and tomatoes. Perhaps she would make chutney. Even though she couldn't abide the stuff. And jam! With fruit picked from her own trees.

There didn't seem to be any fruit trees in the grounds at all, apart from a few caterpillar-clad pear trees that she could see from the bedroom window. They had apparently produced a nice conference pear at one time, according to Ophelia. But now they were so tall it would take a fire crew to pick them.

The gardens needed so much doing, but had so much scope. But Sarah knew she couldn't do everything. She mustn't do too much anyway. It was her first baby, she thought. Their first baby. She was not so young anymore. She would be thirty-four by the time she had him.

Still, they couldn't wait around, not at their age. And they wanted at least one more. Which Sarah secretly hoped would be twins. Her gran was one of twins, so it was possible.

She had bonded to the remnants of the village, namely the Brats and the Plants. In a critical and judgmental world, they seemed to accept her. She was Leo's wife, she lived at the Hall. That was it.

Sarah did wonder sometimes where this feeling of 'everyone else' came from. Who did she see beyond Annie, the staff, the few remaining Crescenters and Leo? The Mangrove family, the Cavalier lawyers, were always turning up with documents, but they were anxious, uneasy, seeming to disapprove of Leo even more than they did of her. And Annie appeared to come nowhere in their calculations, presumably because she wasn't a boy.

And we are on the very fringe of the twenty-first century, thought Sarah. It's amazing!

She was later to realize how much her

feminist indignation about Anya and boys and male lawyers had distracted her from seeing what was really on the collective Mangrove mind, what they had known from the start, that she hadn't.

But for the moment, Disraeli Crescent seemed like home. Mrs Plant was always hospitable, and was fond of Annie in her absent-minded way. Annie was certainly fond of her. She was already running ahead, down the old driveway that once connected the Hall to its village. It was broken and pot-holed now, but it took them through the gloomy, spindly shrubberies, out into the field where the riding stable ponies grazed, down to the little round stone gatehouse and out into the Close. Sarah still found the contrast amazing. The empty moorland to the West of the Hall, the forest of old trees around it; and yet, ten minutes through the tangled shrubberies by the old driveway and the horse-filled field, and she was in the Crescent, in the town itself. The transition between town and Peak Park was as clear and abrupt as that between land and sea. And it would be as long as the awe-inspiring Peak Park Planners continued their reign.

Sarah intended to build some proper stabling in the fields. She was currently in discussions with several local riding schools and farms, and having to evade heavy pressure from Ava about who she made deals with. Ava was all for letting the Home Farm have it for next to nothing, which Sarah privately translated as: next to nothing for the Cavaliers, but plenty of cosy little deals on the side for the Maggses. Cowlishaw sheep already grazed over the large field. Leo had muttered about it at first, but he had to admit it kept the field neat, brought in a little money, and made him feel quite the squire as he looked out over 'his' sheep a'grazing.

Sarah realized these were very small beginnings, basically solving minor problems of keeping the extensive grounds from falling into further dereliction. But it was a start.

She and Annie had now emerged into the Close. The Brat bungalow seemed deserted. Alan would be at his garage, and Flutterby out canvassing somewhere. The boys has just started at pre-prep school, and toddled off every morning in darling little grey blazers with red piping for their three-hour day. Sarah would have liked Annie to go with them, but was stuck until they got something sorted out financially.

Disraeli Crescent, once apparently so quiet that the junior Plants and their friends played tennis in the middle of the road and drew their hopscotch squares in peace, was awash with parked cars, and more cars were coming and going.

The encroaching University and Hospital had turned most of the Crescent into offices and student flats anyway, and once treasured gardens had long disappeared under extension buildings, or practical concrete, or the piles of dustbin bags that students were unable to carry as far as the collection point in the road outside. They could heft them into the gardens apparently, but no further. Only the Plant and the Brat gardens in the little Close still kept their glory.

She held Annie's hand carefully as they negotiated the road and made their way to the backdoor of No. 5.

'Ophelia?' Sarah popped her head round the unlocked kitchen door and found Mrs Plant sitting over two books at her big kitchen table, cutting bread.

'Well, hello there, Sarah and Annie. Come in.' Mrs Plant was always pleased to see you if you came, but never hurt or lonely if you stayed away.

Today, she was wearing a floral skirt with a dusty black polo neck sweater and trainers with white socks over black tights. Her dark grey hair was tied back with something, a bootlace possibly. Mrs Professor Plant had been head of philosophy at the town's redbrick university. And it showed.

'Why not join me for lunch?' Mrs Plant waved them to the kitchen table with the bread knife, scattering crumbs from the enormous doorstep she was cutting. 'Nothing fancy.'

Actually, the Plants used their dining room in the same way they used every other room in their vast stone house, as a space for piling up books.

'Don't even bother with a Sunday roast anymore. Did it all those years for Plant and the children. Anyway, not healthy; so they tell us, don't they?' She cut some more doorsteps, piled cheese on to them, topped them with butter and popped them under the grill.

'What are you reading at the moment, Ophelia?'

Mrs Plant had two books propped up

on the table, one an old worn leather-bound book with a Latin title and the other a paperback with a colourful cover.

'I'm just giving myself a refresher in Descartes, although I don't know why. *Not* a pleasant character. And this is my current Agatha.' Mrs Plant, although long retired from university life, had a passion for her subject and still appeared in various forums pronouncing firmly but kindly on the moral issues of the day. And she also had a passion for Agatha Christie mysteries. She read and re-read them in strict rotation.

'I can remember who did it, I'm afraid. But I can't remember how and why. His alibi seems absolutely foolproof to me. And as for motive! He doesn't stand to gain a penny for a start. Why he should want to kill the woman I do not know … Oh!' She snatched a cloth and began to extract lunch from the grill. 'That reminds me, did you know that Stephan Novak, Varya's cousin, is back in England? He rang me from London yesterday. He has some business to do, but he'll be up here next week. Wanted to know if he can stay with us again. Said yes. Happy to have him. All these empty bedrooms since the children left. We used to be full to the brim in the holidays when the grandchildren were small.'

The bedrooms may have been briefly empty, but they had rapidly silted up with books, and Sarah supposed that this Stephan would have to make a nest somewhere on a pile of them. 'He could stay at the Hall, you know. We may be short of furniture but we aren't short of rooms, and I can always fix him up a mattress or a camp bed. In fact, it would give me an excuse to organize another bedroom.'

'No. He wouldn't even ask to stay at the Hall. He and Leo don't exactly hit it off. He always stayed with us when Varya was alive.'

'Ah. You know Derek Maggs has him down as a jealous suitor rather than a cousin?'

The Plants didn't usually discuss personalities, but establishing who this Stephan was didn't seem like gossip somehow.

'Plant and I see him as a bit of both. He is certainly some kind of distant cousin. They grew up in the same small village, you know, on the Polish/Belarus border. They are all related to each other in some way. Like Wales,' she said mysteriously. 'But, yes, he and Varya were childhood sweethearts, and, if Leo hadn't come along ...'

Sarah couldn't help but think it would have been better if Leo hadn't come along. Presumably Varya would still be alive. But there would be no Annie. And that would be a loss. And she wouldn't be married to Leo now. She no longer knew whether that would be good thing or a bad thing. She decided to stick to more impersonal thoughts and issues and keep herself tranquil at this important time. 'Why Wales?' she asked Ophelia.

'Small country, powerful neighbours, like Belarus. Anyway, Sarah. How is it going? And how's the baby? You don't look any bigger yet.'

'I'm fine. He's fine.' Sarah hugged her stomach. She knew it was a boy. Happiness surged. Of course it was wonderful that she had met and married Leo. He was the best thing that had ever happened to her. She thought of her former life, a single girl in London. Fun, fun, fun, and more dreary fun. She felt depressed thinking about it. What was wrong with her? Hormones, she supposed, as her moods were swinging alarmingly. But marrying Leo was the best thing, the best thing. And when their son was born, that would be the best thing that ever happened too.

She was just so sorry that Varya had

to die, though. To die and to leave a tiny child behind! Varya, I will never let Annie down, Sarah promised her predecessor solemnly. Once poor Leo had his boy he would be able to enjoy both his children. We shall make no favourites. And, ideally, we will give Annie at least another brother or sister. Sarah had spent hours dreaming of a Disraeli Hall full of children and sunshine. And, later, grandchildren. There would be grandchildren. Surely the Plant's big old stone house should be buzzing with them.

'How are all the grandchildren, Ophelia?'

'Plant and I don't see so much of them now. Plant grumbles about it, but I say to him, how many of our precious college days did we spend with our grandparents? Although Plant, bless him, would have if he could.'

Sarah thought of those distant days when an iron curtain had come down across Europe, cutting off the young Polish professor from all his early days. It had been such a strange and a terrible century.

'And he gets so upset about Emily. Isn't it time she got married, and settled down and stopped all this traveling? On and on like that. Wouldn't have minded when he was younger. You realize what a short time you have to spend with the people you love as you get older. Anyway, mustn't bother you with that. Right at the beginning for you.' Mrs Plant sounded rather gruff as she got up to fetch one of her excellent Victoria sponges.

Some of the Plant sons lived locally, and were employed by the education authority or the university or the Peak Park. They were all married and seemed to have a lot of children, who Sarah had never quite got sorted out in her mind. A couple of them had obviously inherited the Plant philosophy gene and were doing heavily academic things at various universities. And there was one son who was in partnership with Alan in The Peak Park Garages, and, like Alan, spent most of his time under cars.

Emily, the only daughter, and the child of their late middle-age, had no interest in academe. She had been working her way round the world as variously a waitress, a cook, a dive-teacher and boat hand for the last five years. Startling postcards would drop through the Plant letterbox at irregular intervals and would be well chewed over at The Coat of Many Colours. Apparently she used to barmaid there now and again.

Sarah bit into her sponge cake. It was filled with home-made jam from the famous Plant raspberries. It was so light she almost felt it needed an anchor to keep it on the plate, Ophelia not having to stint on the eggs. It was a cake from the days of Mrs Beeton. Somewhere, in one of the innumerable cupboards in the back kitchens and sculleries of Disraeli Hall, she might one day come across a strange device. She could take it to the Antiques Road Show when they next arrived in this Northern town, and they would then reveal to her that it was in fact a Victorian Cake Anchor, in super condition, and very rare.

Sarah was eating like a horse at the moment and not really gaining any weight. A side effect of pregnancy that couldn't possibly last, but she intended to make the most of it while it did.

Poor Leo. He was having a difficult time. He alternated between treating her like a delicate porcelain figure, something well worth having valued at the next Antiques thingumabob, and hardly being able to be in the same room as her in case she collapsed on the floor and lost their child there and then. But she understood. He was so worried. He so wanted a son.

It seemed incredibly old-fashioned, all

this inheritance business. But she and Leo had benefited from it. The previous incumbent had had no children at all, let alone a son, and so Leo, a rather obscure cousin, had inherited. If he was to found a new Cavalier dynasty, then he felt he must have a son. Preferably two.

Poor Annie. If only she could have had a twin brother Leo would probably have adored her. Yet, in this day and age, couldn't all these Cavalier traditions of inheritance be overridden by law? Surely Leo himself had inherited through the female line. It had been his mother and not his father who was a Cavalier.

She began to discuss it with Ophelia, wondering if she might know something about the legal ramifications. Which she didn't, but the Plant opinion was very much that Leo needed to have a son for other reasons, those connected with his own childhood. A childhood about which Sarah herself knew next to nothing. The Plants had known Leo as a sullen teenager who had moved into the Coat with his parents. Unusually, his mother had the tenancy, and it was her maiden name – Cavalier – that had gone up over the door.

She wasn't to find out any more that lunchtime either as the conversation somehow changed to hers and Leo's first meeting. 'It had been at a party,' she found herself telling Ophelia. 'The usual sort of thing. Leo had been down at Sotheby's for the last picture sale. I was ready to marry, I had reached that stage in my career, but I wanted to find the right person. Obviously.'

The words echoed softly in the Plant's vast warm kitchen. Tested against stone. And Sarah wondered why she had said them. Is that really what she thought her relationship with Leo had been, a considered, rational thing?

Had she, Sarah Dexter, carefully planned her life as her words suggested? Her career, then marriage in her mid thirties, and a couple of children, followed by a successful return to brilliance in the city? And marriage only and when the right man came along?

Had she spent fifteen years turning down unsuitable men who proposed themselves, and, having met Leo, weighed up his qualities carefully and thought: Yes, this is the one, this is the right time?

Or had her life just happened to her? Had a succession of failed, depressing relationships made the appearance of Leo's golden charm something she could not resist? Had she tried to resist? No. Not once she had realized he was serious. How long had they known each other? A whole two months! That was how considered it was.

Had Leo simply taken her away from all this, rescued her like some fairy prince from childhood bedtime stories? Had she known anything about him at all, let alone made a measured consideration of his husbandly qualities?

What would children's bedtime stories be nowadays? A fairy prince would be quite a different sort of thing, she supposed, and not in the least interested in the beautiful princess. Anyway, beautiful princesses would be too busy kicking bottoms right, left and centre to require any rescue. Dragons would of course be an endangered species, so that any Knight who tried to slay one would instantly fall foul of ...

Sarah's thoughts were interrupted by a roar and a thump as a large black cat suddenly appeared on the table, amidst the mugs.

'Tom. You bad boy. Get down,' said Ophelia ineffectually. The monster paid no attention and stared coldly at Sarah.

'Aaarghh!' Sarah snatched back the hand she had automatically put out to stroke the creature's furry muscular body.

'Tom! You bad, bad boy! Let me get you a plaster for that Sarah. And some disinfectant. I should have warned you. I think he thought you were reaching over to me. He's such a possessive wee thing. And a Very Naughty Boy!' said Ophelia, hastily.

The cat made another lunge at Sarah, and she drew her chair back from the table.

'Oh dear.' Ophelia followed her with the first aid kit, dabbing and bandaging in a practised kind of way. 'He is such a bad boy. You just sit back down Sarah, don't let him bully you. And I'll introduce you. Now. Tom, this is Sarah. And you are to behave. She's my visitor. An honoured guest. I didn't realize you hadn't been introduced yet'.

'No.' Sarah clutched her throbbing hand. 'I'd not had that pleasure.'

'He's fine once he's been introduced, but he's never at home. He's such a roamer, you see.' Ophelia chuckled fondly. 'We did have him neutered, of course, but it hasn't made much difference. He regards this whole area as his territory and likes to patrol. So he's out a lot.'

Sarah was relieved to hear that he was neutered and that there wouldn't be a pride of Boy Toms lurking somewhere out on the moors.

'Oh. Look out!' He had lunged over to Annie's chair. And she had actually touched him. In fact, she was stroking him. She had her precious cheek pressed next to his battered face with its yellow shark's teeth. And he hadn't killed her. Yet.

'Oh, Tom loves children, my dear. He just adores them. Much as Plant and I love him we couldn't keep an animal that would attack a child.'

Ah, of course. Sarah looked at Boy Tom glowering under Annie's attentions. He knew exactly where his adored mistress drew her line, and he was not going to cross it. She wondered if she would be safe now that she had been introduced. Her thumb throbbed, warning her not to take any chances. And she thought that young Annie would be wiser to avoid him after her sixteenth birthday, whatever.

* * *

Another lunch remained vividly in Sarah's mind. Some weeks ago, she had been sitting at the Hall, in the breakfast room, dining off cheese sandwiches and trying to hold yet another slice of Plant cake down on its plate, no Cake Anchors having turned up as yet. She was eating lunch with Debbie and her mum. Wills and Harry had been taken to the park for the afternoon by Alan's parents, who were up for a short visit. Dawn had proved to be a nice lady. And, in the absence of Ava, she and Sarah were able to have quite a few cosy chats about babies.

'I knew our Debbie were a girl right from start. It were way she sat, low like, and I didn't show much. With Scott I was much bigger.' She gave Sarah a professional kind of look. 'It's too early to say with you yet.'

'Oh, I'm sure it's a boy. David.' She patted her stomach, which still seemed as taut as ever. 'I've been sick every morning since, well since, you know. Straight away. And my mother said that she was sick all the time with my brother and never with me. And my granny said the same. She had four boys before she had my mum. She said it was as different as chalk and cheese. Never a day's sickness with my mother. But she said she was sick all the time with the rest of them.'

As she said this, Sarah found herself wondering for the first time about the absence of those far away uncles. They were a lot older than her mother, who was a child of her mother's middle age. But, still, where were they? And their families?

'You know, it's a funny thing.' She got up to take the coffee cups through to the scullery. 'I don't remember ever seeing those uncles once when I was a child.'

'Ah,' said Dawn, taking the cups from her. 'It's them as gives you the most trouble that leaves you on your own in the end. Oh, Ava, you gave me quite a start, standing there so quiet like! Why don't you come and have a sandwich with us? One sandwich won't hurt you.'

Mrs M was in the scullery, without a fag in her mouth for once. If she had been smoking we would have known she was there and wouldn't have said ... Sarah cast her mind back quickly over the conversation. What had they said? What had they been talking about? Pregnancy, babies ... well, Leo had told everyone about the pregnancy, after telling her they mustn't say anything to anyone for a while. And he would probably have told Ava first. Sarah was surprised how sure she was about that. But she did have the satisfaction of knowing it was something Ava hadn't spotted straight away. She did have to be told. A serious lapse, that, in her World of Surveillance. What else had she and Debbie been talking about? They had talked about Sarah's uncles, her missing relatives. No, not even Ava could make anything of that. In fact, if she could turn them up, Sarah might be quite grateful. But she felt a niggling, inexplicable sense of worry. She realized that she was coming to feel it was not safe to give Ava Maggs information of any kind.

Act then, Sarah. Do something, she told herself. Action cuts worry. 'I'm taking Annie into town. We need to get her some new clothes.'

'More clothes! My word, she will be a real little princess by the time you've finished, Sarah. I'm just glad the Cavaliers can afford all this.'

Sarah ignored it. She had decided early and quickly not to play any games with Ava. There really was no point. They were enemies. Not through Sarah's choosing and not because of anything she had done. Apart from marrying Leo.

She wasn't going to go the Manderley route and try ingratiating herself. It wouldn't be any use. And why the hell should I in any case? thought Sarah. If the scrawny old bat doesn't like me being here, tough! But she felt somehow uneasy. As if she had given Ava some information that would have been better not divulged.

And certainly, if Ava Maggs ever chose to give her some advice about which costume to wear at the Ball she would surely soon insist on them holding at Disraeli Hall, Sarah would ignore it. 'But the tenants expect it, ma'am,' said Ava Danvers cunningly in her head. 'And, obviously, it will please Leo no end if you come dressed as Varya, just exactly as she was on the Winter's night that she and Anya left the Hall in such a hurry.'

'Whaay, Mammy, Ah suah will.' The imaginary Sarah now took her part in the conversation, wondering why she had strayed out of Manderley into Tara and become Scarlett O'Hara, with an unconvincing accent. Perhaps it was to annoy the whip-thin Ava by casting her as Mammy? Anyway, she decided, in the eventuality of a Fancy Dress Ball, or what the Americans call a Costume Party, she would come as Ava. In tight blue jeans, multi-coloured hair, lots of woollies, and with a giant fag hanging out of her mouth.

Sarah had meant to cheer herself up with the Manderley/Tara fantasy, but the thought of Varya leaving the Hall that freezing winter's night, with Annie,

and driving so fast down that icy drive
with its lethal bends and encroaching
trees stayed with her, troublingly.

CHAPTER 7

They say that your past life flashes before your eyes as you drown. But it was only her Disraeli Hall life, her Cavalier life, that flashed before Sarah's eyes in all its inevitable detail in that moment when someone turned the light on in the empty Hall. Especially her life there with Leo. She was as blind in the sudden light as she had been in the darkness. She was standing where Leo's murderer must have stood, waiting patiently for the footsteps on the stairs.

She waited for the explosion, the scream, the footsteps, anything. After an immeasurable time, the small hall became visible again. And there was someone standing very close to her, frozen as she had been in that measureless moment.

Now she was going to see the dark at the bottom of the stairs, the piece of the darkness that had detached itself and shot Leo as he screamed in terror and horror and amazement; only the cosmos was playing some sick joke on her. Because Leo himself was standing before her, in a blaze of light. He was standing right in front of her, just where he fell.

Dead before he fell, they reassured her. He didn't suffer at all. He was dead before he fell. He had no time even to scream. And yet he had screamed. Terribly. A scream that still rang in Sarah's ears as soon as the light was turned off.

His leather jacket shone in the kitchen light as he reached his long dead arms towards her. Mercifully, the darkness returned.

'Sarah. Sarah!' Arms, strong and sturdy were holding her tight. She was against broad leather shoulders that would save her from the horror of–

'Sarah. I'm so sorry. You gave me a real fright, too, if it's any consolation.'

Sarah clung to Derek.

'Derek. Oh, Derek, I thought ...' She was too relieved to ask why he was wearing Leo's leather coat. She had been brought back from horror and death and darkness.

'What are you doing here?'

'Hey, I could ask you the same thing, Sarah. I usually do a check round the outside at this time. I just look at the windows, you know. Ever since that night–' He stopped abruptly. 'And I heard footsteps in the hall, just where ...' Derek stopped again. 'I thought, oh ho, what's up? I had no idea you were still here. I thought it must be someone from the household, though. But I kept the lights off just in case.' He held her away from him, looking at her white face. 'You thought ... You poor kid.'

His smile was the most reassuring thing in the world. His arms held her so tightly. Just as her father had once held her after a nightmare, and she had felt so safe. So safe. And then he'd gone. Got tired of them and left. As Leo had left her alone in the dark silence of that terrible night, left her to hear the scream and the footsteps coming slowly, slowly, up the stairs.

'Listen, Leo is dead. He died that night. You know. You saw. We all did. He doesn't walk. You don't believe in ghosts, surely. If there were such things, this house'd be so full of them there wouldn't be room for any of us.'

How odd to be comforted by the assurance that her husband was truly dead! What sort of a wife was I? Because I could stay safe here in Derek's arms forever, thought Sarah dreamily, as his hands pushed the hair gently from her face, and his mouth.

Warmth. And safety. And someone to watch over me, thought Sarah dreamily, as a light switch clicked, and darkness returned to Disraeli Hall.

* * *

Derek walked her to her car. They didn't speak. There wasn't anything to say. Nothing.

They avoided looking at each other, and Sarah drove off quickly. If she had not come in the car, laden with files, would Derek have walked her home to her temporary dilapidated cottage in Disraeli Close? A long, silent walk. Thank you, car. Yet soon it would have to go; and yes, think about that, all the extra difficulty, don't think about what just happened, what should never, never have happened. Never. If she didn't think about it it didn't happen. But that reminded her of other things to be kept from coming into her mind and digging deep grooves there. Put it out of your mind, Sarah, never think about it or refer to it again.

Derek won't. Sarah knew that for sure. He had got what he wanted for so long and he no longer wanted it.

She had no idea how she got home.

She must have picked up Anya. Fed her and put her to bed. Even read her a story. And she had even put herself to bed and gone straight to sleep. It wasn't till she woke up in the small hours of the morning that the dark at the bottom of the stairs came back to haunt her.

She and Derek. Right there. Right where – they couldn't have. No. It was the library, they found themselves in the library. Because moonlight had glinted in at them from tall windows. She could even remember the startled face of the moon. White with shock.

Sarah. How could you? How could you? Certain episodes from the past came back to haunt her. You were supposed to be finished with anything like that, she told herself. Finished.

* * *

It had all sounded so reasonable. All that Victorian repression, all gone. Do what thou wilt shall be the whole of the law. They would have freedom, and windows that were Larkin-high. And so you did what you wanted as long as nobody got hurt.

Only it turned out that you did get hurt. That everybody got hurt.

She wasn't going to sleep now. She got up. She did her automatic check on Anya, who was sleeping peacefully in the second tiny cottage bedroom. She had fallen asleep on her favourite soft toy. Sarah watched her relaxed breathing, the clear gold skin, the ash blonde hair so soft on the pillow. It's going to be different for you, Anya. It's got to be.

You are the only child I am ever going to have. And I am the only mother you have left. And now I have put you in terrible jeopardy. Because if Ava ever found out about tonight ... Sarah shuddered, and went to get herself a cup of tea.

Derek obviously played away.

Obviously. But away. Not at home. And somehow Sarah knew she was something Ava would not forgive. She also knew that she wouldn't blame Derek. She would make his life hell for a while, yes. Use his need to repent and make up and do what he was told to forward whatever scheme she had in hand at the moment. But she would not forgive Sarah. And Ava had Clifford Betts's ear.

Sarah was relying on his lawyers to fight the might of the State and get her Anya. For that, she had given up all claims to anything from Leo's estate. Which as it turned out was not Leo's estate at all. Mrs Jellyby and her fearsome friends now had the full weight of the state behind them, and the Orwellian prospect of 'care' loomed ahead for Anya in Sarah's worst nightmares.

After a last look at Annie, she set off down the narrow cottage staircase to get herself a cup of tea. Sleep did not seem a possibility.

Sitting there, looking out into the moonlit cottage garden, an overgrown tangle that had once been somebody's pride and joy, Sarah found Andy, her first love, coming back into her mind. It had been her first year at college. She had her grant. She was doing well. She could cope with everything, it seemed. The miseries of home forgotten, her life seemed full of possibilities.

And Andy. So sweet he was. Blonde like Leo. But so gentle. And caring. He had wanted an engagement. A marriage as soon as they both graduated. Then a boy and a girl. And a country cottage somewhere. But it wasn't what she had wanted, was it?

But what did she want? What she was told to want? What she thought she ought to want? Excitement? Who knows? A strange mixture of all of those things. But she did go for excitement.

And London. And affairs. If it feels good, do it.

How long did it take me to realize that it *didn't* feel good? So quickly I was in my thirties, so tired of working. So tired of commuting. So tired of bills, bills, bills.

What would my mother have said if I had asked her? I never did though. I never thought she knew anything about anything. What was that joke: When I left home at eighteen I thought my parents were really stupid. When I came back at twenty-one I was amazed at how much they had learned.

'If I had been a child of the Fifties, playing tennis on Disraeli Crescent with the Plant boys and their friends, I would have married Andy.' Sarah surprised herself by saying the words out loud. She sat back in the chair in the dark room, clutching the hot tea gratefully to her. Comforting. It was comforting. She would go and make herself a hot water bottle, and then, maybe, she would sleep.

She glanced into the dark grounds of Disraeli Hall through the little landing window. The trees swayed against the vivid night sky, full of clouds and glimpses of the moon between storm-driven clouds. The rain would start any minute.

Then she froze, glued to the window. A strange beam of light was wavering in and out of the darkness that was the grounds of Disraeli Hall, which lay just beyond the tumbledown cottage garden wall.

Someone was in the grounds. With a torch. At 2.30 in the morning. And it didn't seem at all likely it would be Derek Maggs back again, doing more checks. He ought to be sleeping soundly; the cat that got the cream. And how come he had Leo's Armani jacket? Sarah knew she could never ask him.

* * *

Sarah retched and retched. As sick as a dog.

Serves you right, Sarah. You have made yourself sick. She hung weakly over the toilet bowl, and then shakily got herself back to bed. It wasn't until the sickness had gone on for a whole week of mornings that Sarah realized just how sick she had made herself.

You are pregnant, Sarah Cavalier, she told herself. Pregnant. You are expecting a child. It's Derek Maggs's child. And it's a boy. She knew it with absolute certainty.

If Ava ever found out about this!

CHAPTER 8

Sarah sat in her little cottage in the Close looking out at the Coat of Many Colours, its sign softly singing in the wind. It was a comforting sound in a cold and windy April. The tiny front garden was full of daffodils, as yellow as the Plants' laburnum would be when Spring had really come. As yellow as Leo's hair. Leo would see no more springs. Sarah couldn't stop thoughts she didn't want. It was too quiet. Anya was at her nursery school. The housework was done. She had spent the day being horribly sick. Once again.

Sick in mind as well as body. As if her encounter with Derek at the foot of the second staircase was flooding her mind with so many things she had tried not to think about. Now, with a new life growing inexorably inside her, she had to remember two deaths. She had to get

134

them out of the way, get them over with. The one so close after the other. They could no longer be held in some back attic in her mind. They were bursting out, in all their horror. And all their incompleteness.

Had something similar happened after that weekend when Disraeli himself had stayed at the Hall? There had been rumours of a child then. Could she see Derek and herself as simply parts of an old story, long gone, mostly forgotten?

It was no good. The deaths that she had tried so hard never to let back into her mind were now clamouring for attention. This cold Spring didn't help.

Because Sarah's second Spring at Disraeli Hall came back to her vividly. It had been so different from her first, although once again she seemed to be in the library. Torrents of rain were falling, battering the daffodils that the shrunken Spring was leaving behind. They were tired daffodils, brown round the edges, and it felt cold enough for another frost. As if what had happened had reversed the seasons themselves, and Winter was hurrying back.

Sarah had sat in the library, mulling over what had been achieved in the last year. She must keep herself busy and remember achievements. Not other things.

The Spring bulbs she had planted in the Autumn had mainly done well. But what would a frost do to the tulips that ought soon to be lining the drive with their banners?

I've transformed this room, at any rate, she thought looking round with some satisfaction. The documents were neat and sorted into their carved wooden slots.

How much she knew about the family! More than anyone alive, apart from the dusty Mangroves, who had known so much more than anyone realised.

And she had become a little obsessed

with her predecessor after all. Varya. The first Mrs Cavalier. There were many mysteries about her still. Not the least of them why she and Anya were driving so fast on the moorland road that icy Winter night. But Varya was no Rebecca, although she too had cared for the Hall. She had actually managed to sell the remaining 'good' furniture and got a reasonable price for it. She had even managed to stop Leo squandering it all on fancy cars and holidays abroad. She had ploughed it back into the house, getting a good half of all the unglamorous basics done.

But she had kept the famous Disraeli carver chair, and the bed. Plus the funny old wooden table and chairs in the breakfast room that he was reputed to have breakfasted in, and with very good appetite apparently.

Hardly surprising under the circumstances! He would have had a busy night.

And she had kept the paintings. It wasn't till after she died that Leo had sold them all.

Sarah sometimes even thought that she and Varya could have worked well together as a team, if they could have sent Leo off somewhere. He could have had a year in a fancy hotel, perhaps, with unlimited spending money. A life of sunshine, with nothing mundane intruding. That's what Leo felt he was entitled to.

Be fair, Sarah thought to herself. Be fair. If she hadn't lost their baby ... A little boy too, David Samuel Cavalier ... Those old family names, all gone, along with all their hopes.

Such sadness went through her at the thought of David that she didn't know how to deal with it. They had never talked about it. They couldn't talk about it. She felt as if she had hardly seen Leo since. He had completely withdrawn from her.

Another tragedy in his life, and it was all too much for him. The doctor had told them that Sarah mustn't get pregnant again for a year or so, but then all should be fine. But maybe she wouldn't be able to conceive again. No son for Leo. No siblings for Annie.

In the meantime they had to get down to the basic mundane matter of earning their daily bread. She had still barely been able to take in that Leo simply had no source of income. He seemed to feel that ownership of Disraeli Hall alone conferred a private income and a life of infinite leisure.

And up to now, it had. But all its treasures had been sold off, apart from what Sarah thought of as the Disraeli gear. She had found it when she had ventured through the dusty little trapdoor in the small attic and discovered the grand room she had been expecting. Not packed with furniture, but with those few good pieces safely stowed.

It was Stephan, on one of his regular visits to the Plants, who had told her about the stored furniture, so he must have been Varya's confidant. It hadn't occurred to Leo that they might be worth money. Or to Ava, fortunately. And Sarah was going to keep it that way. She needed something in reserve. Varya had hidden them for good reasons.

The loss of David had allowed Ava back, so how could Sarah help but wonder if Ava hadn't contrived the whole thing? She had assured Sarah she would hold the ladder steady as she took down the old curtains and that Derek would do the heavy work of fitting the new. Sarah remembered the sudden dizziness, and that the ladder had not held steady.

The pain of the loss had never healed between her and Leo. There had been no time, she told herself, because his own sudden and shocking death had followed so quickly on the death of his son. But

140

that line of thought aroused an anger in her that drained her because she could, for the moment, do nothing about it. She needed to keep busy.

She hadn't even tried to go back into her old Yuppie world. She knew her sharpness had long since gone. And she knew that she couldn't face that life anyway, of juggling too many plates while dancing on a tightrope. Just waiting for the crash.

Trading in futures was gambling. Simply gambling. And she had a house and child to support. Not to mention Leo. There weren't many jobs up here, and none that would seem to justify her taking time out from Anya and her duties at the Hall.

'Ava will look after Annie,' Leo had tried to urge her. Hiram Mangrove, of Mangrove, Mangrove and Mangrove, the Cavalier family lawyers, was looking for a secretary, part time, and would pay OK.

'Ava will not look after Annie. At any

time. If I do find a job then it has to pay me enough to put Annie into a good nursery, and the Mangrove job won't even begin to do that. She's already lost one mother. She doesn't need to lose me as well.'

Oddly, Leo didn't argue. Not since the accident. Perhaps something in Sarah's voice warned him. 'Debbie'll be fine with her though, she and her mum. I mean they are here every day.'

'Debbie and her mum looking after Annie is exactly the same as Ava looking after her. In another year Annie will be at school, and then I will think seriously about something. Something full time. In the meantime, I've got the Job Supplement from The Telegraph. For you.'

Sarah made to hand the paper to Leo and he left hastily. He was the Squire of Disraeli Hall, the incumbent Cavalier. He didn't work, any more than Bertie Wooster and his fellow Drones did.

So the money from the paintings Leo was selling when they met and from the sale of Sarah's flat was all that they had. And that still left the problem of the roof! Which had proved to be leaking quite badly after all, though not in the front where the Maggses still slept in comfort.

Varya had brought nothing to the marriage beyond her pregnancy. Apparently there had been a life insurance payout after Varya's death that had long since gone.

Sarah now felt older than Ophelia. And so tired. And given to bursting into tears at the most unlikely moments. No wonder sunny Leo had given her up entirely and seemed to spend his days riding with Ava or Debbie or one of the horsey women from the Home Farm Stables. And his evenings were spent with Derek at the Coat.

Sarah wondered why she didn't especially care, her main feeling being one of relief that the burden of entertaining him didn't fall on her and she could get on with things.

* * *

And now his life was at an end. And Sarah was still here, in the same town, even if no longer the Chatelaine of Disraeli Hall, where she seemed to have put down enough temporary roots to nourish her and ... Sarah shook her head. She didn't want these memories there. She needed to go to bed, to sleep, to stop thinking.

But she had once been woken from a deep and dreamless sleep by the scream, an explosion, and footsteps coming up the small staircase. And found herself alone in the dark. And that was something else that had to be faced. She couldn't keep it locked away any more. It had led to her and Derek, in the dark library. That had shaken everything, changed everything. She was going to be on her own with two small children. And Ava must never know that Derek was the father of one of them. Never. And that meant she couldn't confide in anyone. Not even Ophelia. Derek would never say anything, that was for sure. But she had suddenly become pregnant! How?

Sarah found herself laughing at the ridiculous question. I mean, I have no boyfriend, she explained unnecessarily to herself. Everyone knew that. Leo wasn't long dead and she had been fully occupied with Annie and moving out of the Hall and getting the cottage sorted out. What men had she even seen since then? The dusty old Mangroves? Cliff? Alan Brat? Professor Plant? And Derek.

What was she going to do about this? It was an insoluble tangle as far as she could see. But maybe, to get the present straightened out, she would have to face up to the past and get that straightened out first.

Who had been waiting for Leo and shot him so coldly and efficiently? Whoever it was had begun to walk up the stairs towards her and Annie before something made them change their mind.

And David. Did Ava Maggs deliberately persuade me up that ladder? Did she take advantage of a sudden dizziness? Was it just the accident everybody tells me it was? Suddenly, a long ago conversation with Dawn, Debbie's mum, came back to Sarah. They had been sitting talking about pregnancies, and Ava had been in the small kitchen, standing quietly by the wooden sink with its constant stagnant smell. Not smoking. Sarah remembered her uneasiness, and running back the conversation in her mind. Her pregnancy, which Ava knew about anyway, and her long-ago faraway uncles. There was nothing in that for Ava. Why on earth had they been talking about Sarah's uncles? And, as she thought that, the whole conversation suddenly tumbled out of her memory as fresh and new as if it happened yesterday. They had talked about Sarah's uncles in the context of morning sickness. Just as her granny had been sick every day while carrying her sons, as had Sarah's mum with her only son, so she Sarah knew she was to have a boy as she was being sick every day.

A boy. What she had told Ava was that she was having a boy, the son that Leo had wanted to so much, for so long. Even an Ava Maggs couldn't get round that one. Sarah would have reigned as undisputed queen from then on. If it was no accident, if Ava was truly capable of that, then it made it doubly urgent that she must know nothing about this pregnancy.

But who killed Leo? And why? Why would nobody listen to her, the one who had been there. Why did the Police not listen to her? If it had been Clifford Betts lying there, shot?

How could she protect Annie and the baby and herself if she didn't know who to protect them from? It must have been someone close. Someone very close. Someone who was still here. Nobody broke into the Hall that night. Even the police admitted as much. Why else had they questioned her so fiercely at first? Before they seemed to draw back and wish to drop the investigation as fast as they could.

Accidental death, they said, as did the coroner. An accident. Leo had somehow slipped and shot himself with his own gun. Regrettable. Tragic. But it happened.

No one seemed to wonder what had made Leo go for his gun in the middle of the night. What had he heard? And no one seemed to believe her when she told of the footsteps on the stairs, and the scream.

If she could find out why, then surely she would know who. She would have to do exactly what she didn't want to do: she would have to think clearly and logically about that night. Now. Go over every detail in her mind. She had wanted to put it as far away from her as possible. But the threat remained. And now there was another child to protect. She must think about it again.

But how? How to make herself relive that?

Perhaps she could start with the grave where her golden Leo, once so full of life, now lay. If she could go back to the day of the funeral, with its terrible surprise, then perhaps she might know. And find out whether the killer intended to come back for her and Anya. Yes. Just to remember the day of Leo's funeral would be to remember it all.

CHAPTER 9

The day of the funeral had something of
the horror of the night of Leo's death,
in its own shocking way. The service
had passed in a daze. Sarah could
remember little about it. Leo never
went to church. Neither did she.
Nothing the young lady Vicar said made
any sense or got through the haze. She
remembered how good and quiet Annie
was throughout, solemnly holding
Sarah's hand, looking very serious and
Alice-in-Wonderland in her black and
white dress with its ruffled pinafore.

Did she mourn her father? Sarah could
hardly remember Leo ever speaking to
her.

And Anya had somehow, incredibly,
slept through that terrible night. Sarah
didn't even know how she had explained
to the child why the small staircase,
their staircase, was closed off. Or why

the house was swarming with policemen that morning. She had made very sure that they used the front stairs today though. The day of the funeral.

All Disraeli Crescent had been there to say goodbye to Leo. Professor Plant was looking old and frail. He hung on to Ophelia and they had to sit down during the singing. That got through Sarah's Valium haze. He must be well into his eighties by now. He and Ophelia were the last vestiges of the old world of Disraeli Crescent. When they had gone, what would be left? Not the Brats, as Freddy Ramsbottom had finally taken his heart condition off to a retirement villa in Spain and his Peak Park seat was up for grabs. Flutterby was sure to get in. They were already looking at houses in her expensive new constituency. The occupants of the Crescent and the Close would all be students then, transients, who could make no similar cosy world.

Who would have thought that golden

Leo would be gone before Disraeli Crescent finally disappeared?

The Maggses were there, of course, with Debbie and her mum. Derek looked grim. And startlingly handsome in his neat black suit. She found his presence in the house so reassuring. The Sarah of now thought about the Sarah of then, and how her feelings for Derek had been unacknowledged and unexplained. Unchecked, the seeds of what was to come were already starting to grow. She was relying on his presence. How could she have gone on sleeping in the Hall without knowing he was in the house? Derek meant safety and normality and comfort. Would things have been different if he and Ava had been there that night? It seemed too much of a coincidence that it happened the one weekend they had gone away. Somebody knew. This wasn't an outsider's crime. There was no sign of a break-in. And no sign that Leo had disturbed anybody. He had walked into a carefully prepared ambush. Some noise must have lured him downstairs.

Ava smoked throughout the service and coughed over the grave. Surely churches were automatically non-smoking? But there was nobody there who would dare to check her. The late Autumn sun shone cruelly into her lined face. She had lost even more weight recently and looked startlingly haggard. Astoundingly, she was trying to stop smoking, but not today. Her personality was as vivid and powerful as ever. And Sarah was sure she had already worked out a way to get herself aligned with the new Powers that Be at Disraeli Hall with a view to re-establishing her dominance.

But that's surely me, thought Sarah, with some surprise. She was now the Powers that Be at the Hall. She was the Chatelaine and the mother of the heiress. Well, step-mother anyway. But Ava hadn't come near Sarah, and she didn't even bother with Annie any more. If only Sarah could think straight. Because it was odd. Very odd. If she could think straight, perhaps she could work out why Leo had gone downstairs in the dark. If something he had heard had worried him, he would have woken her. She knew that. She would have been the one to go down.

And she couldn't work out Ava at all. Why wasn't she managing Sarah and Anya now? Or at least trying to? She knew Sarah was pretty Ava-proof, but it wasn't like her not to try. She could surely use Anya to get to Sarah in some devious way that would take her completely by surprise.

That thought added an odd chill to the bleak day, because the formal adoption that she and Leo had finally embarked on was not yet finalized and Anya's future suddenly looked nebulous. After all, with Leo dead, what claim did she have to Annie?

There were some strangers in the back of the church. But they didn't register much with Sarah. Not then.

And there was Stephan. Stephan Novak! What? How? Who had told him of Leo's death? And why was he here? He looked as wooden and unemotional as ever. Short blonde hair, nondescript dark suit. Giving nothing away. Or was there nothing to give away? What was that phrase: a Sphinx without a Secret?

It seemed certain he had loved Varya. And therefore he must at least have disliked Leo, possibly hated him after Varya's death. But hated him enough to ...? He wasn't in the country anyway. She vaguely knew, through the Plants, that he and his brother had brought a Dwor just outside Warsaw, the Polish equivalent of Disraeli Hall in fact. Or was it possible they reclaimed it from Communist appropriation? At any rate, she had heard that they were busy doing it up, turning it into small apartments. Apparently he had also bought a small property in an as yet ungentrified area of London. He had his own concerns, and it could have been the memory of Varya that had drawn him here today; or was he up here on some business connected to his property and just dropped by, as it were? Sarah felt that her head wasn't working properly. Whatever reason Stephan might have for being here, it wasn't because he just happened to be passing. She must still be in shock.

They followed the coffin through the bleak graveyard, passing by the vault where generations of Cavaliers slept the dreamless sleep of death. The dead leaves of November lay all around them, dull and sodden. The blaze of Autumn was over. It was a grey day. Appropriate to the sorrow of a life cut so short, so suddenly.

Sarah was on automatic pilot, the night of Leo's death playing and re-playing itself through her Valium haze. She could think consistently of nothing else. Mechanically, she threw a handful of earth on to Leo's coffin. 'The sure and certain hope of the resurrection.' Sarah shuddered as a gust of cold wind threw the flowers about, tearing their petals. She had given Leo white lilies. The florist had set them among trailing dark ivy. They looked Gothic; redolent of wuthering moorlands and early deaths. And appropriate for a Cavalier funeral.

Anya had chosen her own flowers. Bright red gold chrysanthemums, bringing to the funeral a memory of the blaze of Autumn that the November rains had extinguished.

She had slept through everything. Thank God. Even that terrible scream as the trap had closed on poor Leo. When was the tape going to stop playing and re-playing in her head? wondered Sarah through the cotton wool lining the drugs had put round everything.

She had woken. Something had woken her, abruptly. She was catapulted from a dark and dreamless sleep into a dark and silent room. And an empty bed. She had sat up. What had she heard?

It was a terrible cry. Agony, fear, anger. She couldn't define it. It brought the night to a standstill. Inhuman. An inhuman cry. It sounded like something out of Sherlock Holmes. The Hound of the Cavaliers. Awful. Poor Leo. What had he seen?

Because this cry was more than the shock of finding someone in the dark at the bottom of the stairs. Quietly waiting there, a piece of the darkness suddenly becoming solid.

Leo would have cried out with fear and shock. Yes. Who wouldn't? But the anger, the outrage in the cry. He had known who, or what, it was, in spite of the darkness. Sarah shuddered. What had he seen? Or heard?

The explosion. And then the footsteps,

coming up the back staircase. Quietly, quietly.

Sarah remembered the horror of the game of Grandmother's Footsteps when she was a little girl. Quietly, quietly they would be creeping up on you. You would look round. They would all be still. Stone angels. But so much nearer. The familiar playground, the familiar children all transformed by the menacing stillness. And all the time she was fumbling for the light switch, clicking it and clicking it and nothing. Just the darkness.

She actually felt she had blacked out for a moment. And only the thought of Annie, sleeping in the next room, had pulled her back into the terrible waiting darkness. She threw herself across the empty side of the bed. And, oh Thank God, Thank God, Leo's beside light came on. She pulled all the covers up to herself for protection and looked around the room. Nothing. And no Leo. And silence outside. And something else that she was not remembering.

Because the cry hadn't woken her. She had sat up in bed. Something had woken her, pulled her urgently out of deep sleep. And then she heard the banshee wail. She had heard the cry after she woke up. And the explosion. But there was something else. There was something she couldn't remember.

* * *

They seemed to be heading back towards the few black cars that were silhouetted sadly against the grey Northern sky. She could see Mr Mangrove, the Cavalier family lawyer, talking to two of the strangers from the back of the church. Two men also dressed like lawyers, she would say, if she had to describe them to the police.

How quickly the police seemed to have given up on the case! But why?

Someone had murdered Leo. In his own home. Someone had been waiting for him. Quietly, patiently, in the dark at the bottom of the back staircase. And then they had begun to come up the stairs. For her. For Sarah. And maybe for Anya too. Why hadn't they finished the job?

What had stopped those stealthy grandmother's footsteps? And – a horror that had been with her since that night – what if they came back?

There had been no police protection. Nothing. Not even Disraeli Crescent had seemed to take in the threat implicit in the events of that night. It was as if something had been completed, as if justice had been done. It was over. But they had not heard what Sarah had heard.

Sarah looked back at the grave. The earth lay around it, discreetly covered with green sheets. The flowers were mounded up. They would not last long,

pummelled by this cold Autumn wind.
The gravediggers, who looked alarmingly
as if they had just stepped out of a
Victorian sub-plot, hung around waiting
for them to go. They too were smoking,
but they held their cigarettes behind
their hands, and thin wisps of smoke
blew about among the leaves and petals.
Sarah thought it was the saddest thing
she had ever seen.

She thought back to her gran's
funeral, and then, so close after, her
mother's. Jack, her father, was still alive
as far as she knew. He was somewhere
in Spain with his third wife. And
surrounded by children and
grandchildren. He had no need of Sarah.
And she, who had needed him so much
once, had no need of him now. But she
did desperately need someone to talk to.

Then Derek was at her side, helping
her into the black car. Once again, she
felt protected by his very presence. She
would put up with Ava happily if only he

would stay on. He lifted Annie in beside her and she gave him her enchanting sudden smile. An elderly Cavalier aunt and a dusty cousin from the London branch were travelling with them. They had said nothing on the way to the church, for which Sarah was thankful. She didn't want to be consoled. She didn't even know what she felt, beyond sorrow and pity for Leo. And that terror and horror was waiting to pounce just as soon as this hazy cotton wool feeling wore off. She wouldn't know truly how she felt until she had got over the shock.

'I'm glad you buried him.' The thin cousin in black leant across and tapped Sarah's knee sharply, to get her attention. 'Cremation keeps the hordes at bay,' she waved her spidery fingers vaguely out of the window at the stone terraced houses, 'but Cavaliers should go in the family plot. Pity the Mausoleum is full.'

Sarah shuddered. The Mausoleum was

truly horrible, and, even if there had been space, she felt sure her golden Leo would not have wanted that. She would have preferred cremation herself. But apparently it was not for Cavaliers.

'Now.' The thin cousin tapped Annie equally sharply. 'You should have been a boy, young lady. Poor Leo. He would have died happy if he knew he had secured the inheritance.' This last remark was addressed to the dusty cousin and they began a long rambling talk about Cavaliers and wills and who might inherit now.

That pierced through the cotton wool surrounding Sarah's head. She felt so angry on Annie's behalf, although Annie, watching them wide-eyed, seemed almost on the verge of bursting into giggles. Anya was going to be a child of the twenty-first century after all. And these were the few remaining relics of the Nineteenth.

'I'd have had Leo cremated if he

hadn't specified otherwise. Ridiculous waste of perfectly good building land, all these cemeteries.' Which wasn't exactly Sarah's opinion, but she wanted to annoy them as much as they had annoyed her. And it felt good to be alive again. And to feel something other than fear and sadness. 'And it's ridiculous in this day and age to say that only a son can inherit. No court in the land is going to uphold that.' Here Sarah felt on firmer ground, but she would not have stated it so baldly if she hadn't been provoked.

* * *

When Mr Mangrove seemed happy that all who should be there were assembled, he began to cough and to rustle the enormous will. Annie still held Sarah's hand. And said nothing. Sarah glanced round. Who was here? In the old library, some rather bleak refreshments set out by Ava. It was odd to see so many people here. A vivid picture came to her of their plans to fill it with sons and daughters. Poor Leo.

Oh no, she pleaded with herself, don't let me start breaking down now. If she could just hang on until she was alone, all this formal business over, and these people gone. Then she could break down, privately. After getting Annie to bed. After sorting out the problem of whatever to do with the Hall. How to keep it going, for Leo's and Annie's sake. Or would it be a question of selling it, if the will allowed her to? There would seem to be no other possibility. She and Anya could probably live on the proceeds of the few remaining good pieces of furniture, perhaps even sell off all the old books and documents and paperwork. But what would be the point? With the Hall crumbling around them. If they sold, there should be enough for a small house, a small income, and something put aside for Anya when she was twenty-one. Unless they could persuade the Peak Park planners to relent and sell off some fields. She and Leo had been discussing that only the night before, the night before ... Sarah's mind had pulled her back to the darkness of the second staircase yet again. And she must not think about that. She must get through this will reading. They would be OK, she and Annie. And once she was at school, Sarah could retrain. Maybe as ... Who were all these people?

She looked round, while Mr Mangrove droned on through his heretoforeafters and partiesaforementioneds. She registered the Brats. Alan and the twins were all as neat as new pins in black suits and ties and polished shoes. Wills and Harry look so sweet we would want to take their photos if this wasn't a funeral, Sarah thought, disconnectedly.

Flutterby was splendid, in a black wool

suit, with heavy gold jewellery scattered at optimum points. Her hat was dull gold with a silky black ribbon, and her curls were suitably and seriously confined within it. Oh, and her shoes! What they must have cost!

Derek and Ava were there. Of course. Derek looked ... anxious? Worried? He seemed to have lost his usual cat-like self-containment. Perhaps he had been really fond of Leo. Ava was head to toe black. She looked more like the widow than Sarah did in her neat and understated grey. Almost theatrically so. She looked as haggard as she had in the harsh wintery light at the graveside. Yet she has almost an excited air about her; expectant, thought Sarah. She looks expectant.

Well, fair enough. It was possible Leo had left them something. Although she couldn't imagine what, even if he had wanted to. The Cavalier inheritance just passed on to the next Cavalier. Her and then Annie. And she would have to sell

Disraeli Hall. What option did she have, really? Their jobs were at stake, which would probably explain Derek's anxiety.

There were the unpleasant Cavalier cousins from the car. But they were distant old relics, Leo and his family had precedence as far as the Hall went. And there was Debbie and her mum, two more who would lose their jobs.

But what did Leo have to leave beyond the Hall? There was no income, no life insurance. And be fair, Derek and Ava were fond of Leo. As he was of them. They were his friends really. All of them here. Probably more than she ever was. The thought surprised her.

But who were those people at the back? That woman, and the two men in black with her. And a young girl. In a very short black skirt, and with a sulky look on her face. She was dressed in the provocative way of twelve-year-olds these pre-millennium days, but still looked touchingly young.

The men looked like lawyers. But whose? Well, no ... one looked more like he could audition successfully for the next Mitchell brother in EastEnders. But the other one did have a legal look about him. He looked more like the sharp twenty-first century American lawyer, though, not the dusty Victorian kind that Leo had favoured. Maybe she was going to meet some of Leo's elusive friends at last!

Mr Mangrove was just getting to the point, when the woman at the back stood up. She was about to say something. How could I have missed noticing her, if she was at the church? wondered Sarah. She certainly wasn't at the graveside.

The stranger was tall, with long, elegant legs. Her face was model perfect apart from the creases of the heavy smoker around the brow and eyes. Her mouth was as sleek as a sword slash, all her features were chiselled and cut to perfection. She would be a marvel to photograph. No bad angles. Of course. Because as it was going to turn out, she had been a very promising model when marriage had cut her career short.

Her hair was black as night. She was like a poem. Byron, wasn't it? She walks in beauty like the night. 'Like twilight too her dusky hair.' Or maybe Tennyson? 'A perfect woman, nobly planned, to warn, to comfort and command.'

But not twilight hair. Midnight. Hair as black as midnight, as black as the dark at the bottom of the stairs. She wore a bright red Chanel jacket over a short black dress. And, it seemed to Sarah, her dress alone reflected the tragedy that had brought them here.

The image of Leo, lying in pools of bright red arterial blood at the foot of the servant's staircase, was forced into her mind.

Briefly. Because the apparition – Donna, as it turned out – spoke. Her flat

Essex voice was so incongruous that Sarah found herself looking round to see who was speaking, drowning out the upmarket model beauty who was standing up in front of them all moving her mouth.

'I am Mrs Cavalier, and I claim my inheritance.'

She couldn't have used those words, could she? Come on down, Mrs Cavalier. Take the Money, or Open the Box. Who Wants to Marry a Millionaire? Sarah found herself refusing glasses that were pushed at her mouth. People were hovering, offering her tea, whisky, anything. None of which she wanted.

'Come along, Sarah, a nice cup of hot tea with plenty of sugar, that's the thing for shock.' Sarah took the tea from Ava Maggs and drank it. She needed it now. She had just suffered a second shock. Mrs M was not surprised at all. She knew. And she was enjoying every minute of it.

CHAPTER 10

'A nice hot cup of tea. And I've put some of Plant's whisky in it.' Sarah gulped it down thankfully. It even tasted consoling, unlike Ava's microwaved hemlock.

'Anya! Where is she?' Sarah could remember clutching tightly at Annie's hand, as Annie had clutched at hers, but couldn't remember much else beyond Ava's triumphant eyes, and suddenly finding herself in the Plants' enormous kitchen.

'She's fine.' That was the professor. 'She's in the lounge cutting out her paper dolls. Come through and we'll be comfortable.' But Sarah couldn't imagine anything more consoling than being in the Plants' farmhouse kitchen. Warm and cosy, heated by its enormous old kitchen range, it protected her from the bleak Autumn outside.

'His name wasn't Cavalier, you know. He was a very distant cousin. He changed it. And I think that's how he must have got away with this. It was considered quite a thing on the Crescent on those days, that he, his family, were using the wife's name. But we never asked about it. You didn't then, somehow. But he must have reverted to the original name when he married this Donna.' Ophelia briskly cut up one of her cakes. 'We'll have something to eat and talk this through.'

Professor Plant still looked dazed. And frailer than ever. 'I just can't take it in. Leo. Lee, should I say. We always knew him as Lee Cavalier. A darling little boy he was, too. So sweet and sunny. But his mother was a difficult woman. He wasn't allowed to play out with the other children. And he had to go to elocution classes, poor child. I was always surprised she let him come over here to see the boys; thought she would have been worried about him catching my accent!'

'Ah, no, Plant.' That was Ophelia, authoritative. 'Foreign accent no problem, but any slight hint of what they were so eager to leave behind in his voice ... No, she wouldn't have stood for that.'

'What about Leo's dad, then? He never once mentioned him, you know. Not once. And I always supposed that he had died when Leo was young. We both seemed equally bereft of fathers.'

'Well, Sarah, he did what he was told, basically. He was a nice person, but a quiet man. Anything for a quiet life. And she ruled the roost. So in a way, Leo didn't have a father.'

Ophelia passed more cake. Everyone seemed to be eating heartily. Perhaps because they still could. Because they were still alive. Because life was so precious.

'But he and his mother were very

close. Very close. All her hopes were pinned on him. I think he must have married Donna just after she died. Mrs Cavalier would not have approved of her at all.'

The professor crumbled his cake thoughtfully so that his plate would have required a thousand little cake anchors, had any Victorian got round to inventing them. 'What about his marriage to Varya, then? It wasn't a marriage at all! And what about Anya?'

Sarah was just taking in gratefully that whatever Ava may have known, the Plants were as surprised as she was. And how about Derek? Had he known all the time? And Ava Maggs. Sarah suddenly felt certain that Leo would have told her everything. She would have extracted every last secret from him. But would she confide in her husband? Probably only as much as she needed to.

'I'm trying to put this together.' Ophelia looked keen and serious. Sarah felt that she was internalising Miss Marple at this point, or perhaps the great Hercule himself.

'Are all your little grey cells fully engaged?' she asked. They laughed. And hastily stopped themselves. 'It's all right,' Sarah reassured them. 'What is there to do but laugh? For all that, I am so sorry about poor Leo. He did love life.'

And he did. He relished it. But he never loved her. Face up to it. He loved the function she could have performed, giving birth to his son. But once she failed, that was it. And if Sarah was to provide money for his lifestyle, she had failed at that too. Well, once the money from her flat had been spent. Yes, in retrospect, their honeymoon period had lasted as long as the money did, and no further. But there had always been the possibility of a second honeymoon if she produced the required son and heir.

And there was something else to face. Why should Leo have loved her when she didn't love him? She admitted it fully to herself at last. She had loved him briefly for his glow, his charm, for those few wonderful weeks they had. But she didn't know him. And when she got to know him, she didn't love him. She didn't even like him very much.

Did she ever even really know him, though? She was never even married to him, as it turned out.

It was a stupid story she had told herself, that she'd waited till the 'right' one came along. The truth was she had wanted to be married, she had desperately wanted a child. She had wanted to get away from the career girl rat race. Leo was so charming. And he wanted what she wanted. And he was returning to the North, so he had – oh dear – taken her away from all that.

If David had been born, what would have happened then? He'd have been orphaned so young, Sarah thought with a shock. There would have been yet another child to grow up without a father.

'So what was Leo's name originally?' Sarah wondered why, of all the questions going round and round in her head, that one popped out.

Ophelia hesitated. 'I think it was Skittle, Skittles, something like that. His mother made his father change the name to Cavalier when it began to look like there was a chance Lee might be the inheritor of the Hall. It was her mother's maiden name. They changed it just after they took over the Coat. A long time ago. She had Cavalier put up over the pub door right from the start, though.'

'Skittles. Leonard Skittles.' How different that sounded from Leo Cavalier.

'No. Lee. Lee Skittles.'

'Lee.'

'The English caste system is a subtle and complex thing and difficult for foreigners like myself to follow.' That was the professor, happy that he could now find a footing in the conversation. 'Lee and Leo. Even I can understand that that one letter makes all the difference.'

So she had been married to Lee Skittles. Only she wasn't. He was never married to me. But why? Why on earth hadn't he divorced the dazzling apparition in her blood red jacket? This was hardly Jane Eyre, after all.

'He thought she would come back to him when he became the Lord of the Manor!' Somehow Sarah knew she was right. Leo had loved that strange woman in red, with her model beauty and her flat voice. 'He thought he could get her back.'

So Leo could love. And he had loved. But certainly not Sarah. And probably not Varya either, or he would have loved Annie, whatever.

'Well, yes. They obviously got married very young, before there was a real chance of the inheritance. Donna Skittles, Donna Cavalier.' Ophelia pronounced the names thoughtfully. 'Why did they never divorce? I wonder if later she was very keen that Prue would be sure to get the Hall.' She stopped herself suddenly. If, as it now seemed, Prue was the only legitimate child Leo had had, Ophelia would probably feel that this was not the right moment to speculate about it and inheritances. And not the right moment to wonder where Anya might now stand.

Sarah was only just taking in the fact that Leo had another child, first born, a legitimate child, when the doorbell rang. The back door, so it was someone local, someone who knew. Sarah braced herself. If it was Ava Maggs, she was going to have to be careful. A jury might not see one Valium tablet as an excuse for losing control and attacking the woman. But it was the Brats, still resplendent in full funereal outfit. With

Wills and Harry, who disappeared off to the lounge to find Anya. The Plant house was a paradise for children, being enormous, far from neat, and crammed from cellar to attic with books and interesting old things.

Boy Tom had stalked in with them and sat possessively in front of Ophelia, impeding her attempts to eat cake. Even the cake was getting the 'She's mine, keep off her' look, Sarah noticed through her haze.

What had this Donna said when someone had tried to commiserate with her on her husband's death? Something to the effect that someone, whoever he was, had done her a favour? That might be admirably honest, but it didn't make any sense. If she had wanted a divorce, then surely, in this day and age, she could have got one whether Leo agreed or not. She would hardly have had to be frightened, not with the boyfriend/bodyguard she had. Because the big bruiser, the missing Mitchell brother, had moved forward and put his arm round her at that point. If anyone looked like a murderer, he did.

Had he done her the 'favour'? Who will rid me of this troublesome husband? But why? Why? It must be something to do with the inheritance. And what about the male entail? Prue was another daughter, after all.

'He's getting impossible! He won't even let me knit of an evening now.'

Confusingly, that was Ophelia on the subject of Boy Tom.

'Needs a good kick of his furry backside.' Professor Plant stroked Tom dotingly.

Tom tolerated the professor for Ophelia's sake, as he tolerated children below a certain size. And they would never ask anyone to rid them of their troublesome cat.

'Mind you,' said Ophelia, giving in and allowing Boy Tom to leap on her and be cradled in her arms, 'he's as adventurous as ever. He still does his rounds of the neighbourhood, and I can cram in a bit of knitting then.'

She always had jumpers for the many Plant grandchildren on the go, on various needles that she juggled with great skill, despite the touches of arthritis beginning to curve her fingers and thicken her wrists.

Flutterby had removed her hat and carefully re-arranged her hair and, while Alan discussed all the possible routes The Real Mrs Cavalier (or Skittles) could and should have taken from London, she kept up a background commentary about Prue. Who looked big enough to be out working, or studying full-time, not gallivanting half way across England to go to funerals. She certainly dressed like she was at least eighteen. And was in fact an able-bodied young woman, so Sarah deduced.

Flutterby seemed subdued, though.

Donna had obviously been a shock to her as well. And when the Brats had got road maps and able-bodied youngsters out of their system, they too joined in the general chorus of amazement and speculation.

Sarah was so relieved that her Disraeli Crescenters hadn't known about Leo and his marital arrangements any more than she had that she decided to dismiss the problem of Donna and Prue from her mind and think about it tomorrow.

After a while, as Ophelia and Flutterby were organizing the next cups of tea, they drifted down the long Plant corridor to the enormous lounge where a log fire roared. And there Sarah received her last shock of the day. Annie, Wills and Harry were sitting round a stocky, blonde man, who was reading from the latest Harry Potter in carefully enunciated English.

Stephan. Of course. He would be staying with the Plants. He always did.

But that brought back the question of why he had come to Leo's funeral. The only answer that came to Sarah was the rather sad and gruesome one, to make sure Leo really was dead. But also perhaps to visit Anya and make sure she was going to be OK. After all, Annie was the last of Varya, so to speak.

She was now an important child, in fact. Leo's sole heir. And no Victorian stuff about male entailment could actually change that. Sarah had already had some brief consultation with a solicitor in town. And was prepared to hire him if necessary. And worry about how she was going to pay him later. No, that wasn't right. She tried to get the Valium cotton wool out of her head. Because that was all finished now. Anya wasn't the heir. Neither she nor Varya had actually been Leo's wives.

Donna was the mother of Leo's true heir, the sullen Prue. A typical teenage girl, it seemed, sulking because she hadn't wanted to come with her mother to the funeral. Sullen, with a bad skin. She had none of her parent's beauty as yet.

And how did she get from the graveside to the Plant's kitchen? Sarah wondered as she sipped at another piping hot cup of tea. She could remember the funeral in bits and pieces. The forlorn grave. How awful it had been to leave sunny Leo there. Biting sharply at the callous Cavaliers in the car. And Ava Maggs's gloating eyes as the real Mrs Cavalier spoke.

Then she was in the Plants' kitchen, and now, suddenly, she was sitting by Ophelia and Boy Tom, sipping tea, and looking out over the familiar vista of the Plant rockery and the peach tree that the professor had amazingly coaxed to grow and fruit in this cold Northern town.

'Good afternoon, Mrs Cavalier. My sympathies to you and Anya.' Stephen enunciated the words with his usual care and shook her hand in the Plant manner, which made her hand feel kissed.

'Stephan. Hello. I'm afraid this isn't a happy occasion for us to meet again. And actually I'm not Mrs Cavalier as it turns out. I'm still Sarah Dexter.'

As Sarah said those words, a feeling of relief flooded her. She was still Sarah Dexter. So she could wipe the slate clean and start again. Deceptive Autumn sunshine polished the last few leaves of the peach tree. It wouldn't last. Winter was on its way. And it would come early to Disraeli Hall.

* * *

Vivid as the day of the funeral was, it provided no clues. But it had provided more mysteries to ponder.

Some weeks later, Sarah sat in the back kitchens of Disraeli Hall, no longer her or Anya's back kitchens, chewing it all over with Dawn and young Debbie. They all sat as close to the gas fire as they could. Debbie had quite forgotten she didn't like Sarah, and was full of this new 'stuck-up' Londoner who had appeared, apparently to claim the Hall.

'She's been walking round here just like she owned the place, her and that stuck-up Prue. Not a word to us. Just walking round measuring things. And picking things up. I followed them all the time, Sarah. I wouldn't trust them one inch.' Debbie seethed with pleasurable indignation. 'Her and her jodhpurs.' This was a scornful reference to Prue, and definitive evidence of her lack of ability to be one of the people. She seemed to Sarah to be the typical horse-mad teenager, whose sulky manner probably came from insecurity and shyness rather than arrogance. She appeared to be living over at the Home Farm Riding Stables, where she had joined the groups of horsey young girls following Maria O'Connell about dotingly.

Maria was Ava's best friend. They both had the same weather-beaten leanness, but Maria seemed straightforward, if alarmingly abrupt. The sort who prided herself on speaking her mind, calling a spade an expletive undeleted spade every time. But at least you knew where you were with her. Pouting Prue adored Ava, too, and asked her endless riding-related questions, hanging on to every word of her answers.

Though Donna, her consort Shug and Prue seemed to be left unsupervised in Ava terms, as Sarah was. They were of no importance now as it seemed clear that neither of Leo's surviving wives would inherit, even though one of them was the mother of the legitimate heiress. Clifford Betts, the last and briskest of the male Cavaliers, had made his appearance and his decisive claim to Disraeli Hall. It had been his solicitor, sleek and twenty-first century, who had been standing at the back of the library, watching Donna make her bid for the Hall.

CHAPTER 11

'Thank you very much, Stephan.' Sarah
found herself gushing as she tried to
get past him in the tiny kitchen to make
the tea she had promised. If only she
was still mistress of Disraeli Hall it
would all be easier, she thought. At
least there would be some physical
space between them. They wouldn't
have been cramped so awkwardly in
this tiny, cold cottage.

The trees in the tangled garden
outside the kitchen window were fast
losing their leaves, and the red-gold
background provided by the tall trees of
the Hall was already fading. She
commuted to work every morning
through the shrubberies, still overgrown,
still awaiting Clifford's bulldozers, past
the Home Farm horses in the Cavalier
fields, and spent her mornings in the
library sorting Cavalier papers. It was a

pleasant enough routine. She never saw Ava, who didn't believe in wasting time on anyone who had no influence, nothing that could be put to any practical use. Nor to her relief did she ever see the First Mrs Cavalier. Apparently, she, Shug and Prue were being put up in the guest wing of Cliff's mansion in the Home Counties. She was sure they had been promised something more, though, come the re-development. Why else would Donna have given in without a fight when Clifford's team of lawyers struck, with their legal insistence that the Hall belonged to him, and had done all the time? She was a forceful lady; but not of course in legal terms.

Annie had started school, but happily spent her holiday mornings at the Brats playing with Wills and Harry. Sarah, who had no social life now, reciprocated by being a constant and reliable babysitter, so Flutter and Alan could attend their many functions.

If only she could get Anya's adoption finalized, and if she could keep her job with Clifford. And if she could stay in this cottage. She was paying no rent at the moment: her price for leaving the scene with no legal complications was a free, if rather decrepit, home rent-free for the moment, a part time job, and legal help with the adoption of Anya. Surely the Disraeli Country House Hotel would have something for her, something part time?

Sarah watched Stephan carefully drinking his tea. He was good looking, but with none of Leo's charm and flash. He had presumably come round to see Annie, the last he had of Varya. She wondered if she ought to ask him to come with her to the little school to pick Annie up; or would he think she was just angling for a lift? 'Shall I come with you to pick up Anya from school?' he asked, neatly sorting that one out, and they set off to drive to the little nursery down by the shopping centre.

Stephan had loved Varya, Leo had loved Donna, her father had loved his son and his new wife and children, her mother had loved her father and never stopped pining for him, but who had ever loved ...

She stopped herself. Anya loved her and she loved Anya. And she had found a kind of family on Disraeli Crescent. Which ought to be enough for anyone.

CHAPTER 12

The Millennium Eve had come and gone leaving Anya and Sarah in the tumbledown cottage on Disraeli Close. It was Clifford's cottage, of course. His Dream Team of Lawyers would let her stay there until they had defeated the planners and the time came for the full re-development. She had left the Millennium unmarked, beyond watching it come in on the telly round with Ophelia, the professor and quite a lot of children and grandchildren.

And it had become a regular thing to join them for lunch and the TV news on Fridays when she finished work at the Hall. The Weather was almost a sacred ritual round at the Plants. Sarah knew better than to try and talk through it. She found it rather comforting. She felt that the Plant children had had a childhood of regularity and ritual, and that she was seeing the very last glimpses of it. She wondered how much different her own life might have been if she too had had some degree of … But her thoughts were interrupted by the commencement of the Ceremony, which she now took as seriously as she was expected to. Both Plants sat forward tensely in their chairs as the weather girl and her charts appeared. It was the pretty Irish girl today, the one the professor especially liked. She pointed at her charts a lot and mentioned a great variety of weather they might expect the next day.

'Sun, but the possibility of rain,' said Ophelia thoughtfully. 'But there could be high winds, though probably not snow,' countered the professor tensely. They talked it through for a while, and agreed how accurate Ms. Weathergirl's forecast had been for today.

It must have been similar to today's, then, thought Sarah, who never watched the Weather unless she was with the Plants. It had started out cold and rainy and misty, had become sunny later, then the wind had bought clouds; but no light scatterings of snow. Just an ordinary English day, really. Like most English days. How fortunate the Plants were to get so much excitement out of their forecasts.

The news followed, which they watched, too, but it lacked the sacred quality of the Weather, and you were allowed to talk while it was on. The local news followed, and Clifford got a mention, but then he usually did. Apparently Hello! had done a spread on the Southfork Mansion that he had built somewhere in the South of England. It was also going to feature in Through the Keyhole.

Sarah wondered about Through the Keyhole at Disraeli Hall. She wouldn't put it past Clifford to arrange some similar publicity for the Hotel once it opened. But what about B.C. – Before Clifford? When the Hall was still much as it had been when Benjamin Disraeli spent his weekend there? What would she have seen through the keyhole that weekend? And on the night when Leo was killed? If she had been able to look through the keyhole from the library corridor into the dark at the bottom of the stairs would she have seen only darkness? And then a piece of the darkness detaching itself from the rest, coming alive? She would have heard a scream, a scream of complete and utter outrage, an explosion, illuminating – what? Could it possibly have been Clifford himself? Sarah shuddered, and quickly returned to the soothing local news programme before the footsteps on the stairs began their climbing in her head. Anyway, one thing she could be sure of: it would not have been Clifford Betts she saw. He always hired people to do whatever had to be done. Anyway, why would he have done anything like that? His claim was perfectly good, perfectly legal, outweighing the Skittles' claim easily as it turned out. He would only have needed a slick flick from his Dream Team of Lawyers to get Leo and Sarah out of the Hall. So why hire a hitman?

Flutterby was on again, too. She had a lot to say about getting the able-bodied youth of the city back to work once she was elected, and then she had a little speech pointing out all the flaws in the Councillor Albert Cowlishaw Tramway, which was obviously written by Alan.

'He was such a darling little boy, very solemn. You just wanted to pick him up and cuddle him.' That was Ophelia, taking them back to earlier days in Disraeli Crescent. Sarah gathered that she meant Albert the Tramway, not Alan, although she had known them both from childhood.

'Yes, he and Emily used to play tennis

on the road out there.' Professor Plant gestured to the road, which was not wide and was choked with cars parked on both sides. It seemed worse than ever this evening, Sarah thought.

'No, it wasn't Emily, it was–' And here Mrs Plant named one of their many sons. 'By the time Emily came along there wasn't anywhere left to play outside of the garden. The roads were so dangerous for a child even then. And the bomb sites had long gone. And the building sites, in the centre. Even the local parks weren't what they were once they got rid of the park keepers.'

'Simply letting people walk on the grass was probably retrograde in the long run. Though it shouldn't have been.' Professor Plant sighed for the brave new world they had hoped to build from the rubble and bomb sites of World War Two.

As if on cue, Councillor Albert Cowlishaw himself appeared on their screens to talk about other worlds. He was sturdy now rather than sweet, with legs that were definitely made for hiking. Surely he would see trams as the soft option. Sarah thought that a more fitting namesake tribute for the Councillor might have been an especially harsh and hardy moorland walkway. One that would have a high rate of attrition, with many cairns standing as silent memorials to the walkers who had given up and caught the tram home.

'He and Emily were very close for a while. He was quite cut up when she decided to leave.'

'Until Flutterby turned up,' Professor Plant reminded his wife.

'Of course she was a gorgeous young girl, as you can well imagine, Sarah. They met at Emily's leaving party and it was love at first sight'.

Confusingly, they were now talking about Alan Brat. They seemed to have known everyone as a child. Even Leo, although they had never talked about him much.

Which was fine with Sarah. Who anyway was wondering why Councillor Cowlishaw hadn't been the first story on the news, rather than Flutterby, as he was a very important story indeed. He was being besieged by the world's media, who must have arrived in force in the city. It seemed they had been jetting in from the far corners of the earth. Maybe that would account for the unusual number of cars in the Crescent.

Because it seemed that, to mark the Millennium, Councillor Cowlishaw had been kidnapped in broad daylight from the streets of his own city by an alien spaceship, taken off somewhere in the general direction of Betelgeuse and returned. He wasn't kidnapped from his Tramway at least. That would have been an especially bitter pill to swallow. And, in contrast to all other such abductees, he had appeared back on earth clutching a genuine alien artefact, an object whose substance was now baffling the whole scientific world. And something very strange had been placed on his head.

Sarah and the Plants stared at various representations of the artefact. It was vaguely knife-shaped, but obviously not a weapon as it was light and lattice-worked. Machine-carved, or so the current scientific consensus would have it. And it had what appeared to be hieroglyphics on it. The world's Scientific Community was united in a frenzy of translation.

It was all rather a tragedy for the world's media though, because clamour as they might round Councillor Cowlishaw, they hadn't managed to get anything out of him yet other than the words, 'I thought it were a bit odd, like.'

'Well, at least we know he's not been replaced by an Alien Being.' That was Ophelia. 'They'll get nothing more out of our real Albert,' agreed the professor with a certain grim satisfaction.

And I got nothing out of my marriage. Nothing, thought Sarah. Although if I can just hold on to Anya, I will at least have something worthwhile to do, someone to care for. Someone to love. I will not forget my pledge to Varya.

The Media clamoured on as a background to her sad thoughts. There was an election coming up, and Albert had woken up to his opportunity and was now politicking away like mad. Which wasn't exactly what the world's media wanted. He was even claiming that things such as alien abductions could be done away with by a simple by-law if the good citizens would only return his party to power.

Could anyone, anywhere, still really believe in politics? thought Sarah. What haven't we tried? What is there that hasn't failed to work for us? If we can't even make the trains run on time, or the hospital queues shrink, what chance do we have against alien abductions?

Albert Cowlishaw's electioneering diatribe about the sins of his lib-dem predecessors was interrupted by a shriek of BREAKING NEWS, and a mouthful of linguists came on to announce the beginnings of a breakthrough with the hieroglyphics. Apparently the first words were definitely adjacent to the verb 'to give' or 'to present', and it looked like there was some kind of location signifier involved.

'A Present from Betelgeuse!' shouted Ophelia and the professor at the screen. But it was obviously going to take them ages to work it out.

'He's been on a day trip to Betelgeuse and brought back a souvenir letter opener and a kiss me quick hat. He was never one for anything fancy, if you know what I mean. So cuddly, though.' Ophelia sat back lost in thoughts of the past, as the new Millennium hurtled

them forwards into a future that could
not long include her and her professor.

CHAPTER 13

How Spring had advanced while she wasn't paying attention! It seemed to be turning itself into Summer at high speed. Professor Plant's laburnum was in full bloom, its clear saturated yellows glowing in the gentle twilight. And was that Flutterby perched elegantly on the wall underneath the tree, her silk sheath perfectly matching the laburnum?

Yes. She and Professor Plant were deep in talk, murmuring together in the evening garden. Flutterby's exquisitely carved profile was close to the professor's ear; her impossibly long dark lashes almost brushed his cheek. They often spent the lighter evenings in this way, companionable under the invisible moon, deep in serious and philosophical conversation.

'Darling Plant, you simply cannot allow

able-bodied young men, who are perfectly capable of doing a good day's work, to lie in bed till–'

Professor Plant did not espouse the Gradgrindian Liberalism of Flutterby, his politics being of an altogether more romantic nature. Sarah could picture him, cloak flowing in the wind, cavalier hat with its fearless feathers fluttering, sword in hand, defending his beloved NHS as it began to go down before the advancing tanks of the Millennium, much as the old trees of the Hall were going down before Clifford Betts's bulldozers.

Come to think of it, those tanks and bulldozers would probably be driven by Flutterby's able-bodied young men, bitter at being ousted from their beds before the crack of noon.

As she walked past the Plant front gate she could glimpse Ophelia through their tall stone dressed windows. She was tucked up on the sofa with their fierce old Tom, happily absorbed in her latest Agatha. Boy Tom opened one green eye. Even through the glass, Sarah could feel the force of, 'She's Mine, You keep off Her, or else'. Her thumb throbbed and she hurried out of his view. And there, just round the corner of the Close, was Derek Maggs, and a shadow retreating into the distance. Was it a Debbie-shaped shadow? Sarah hoped not. For a variety of reasons.

She felt she was getting large and clumsy now. And Derek never came near her. Thankfully, there was no reason for them to meet. The Maggses remained at the Hall. Still in their privileged bedroom. It had become obvious that the Betts lawyers had been tunnelling away like the moles in the old walled vegetable garden, undermining everything. The Mangroves had felt the vibrations, seen all the insecurities of Leo's position, but had been paralysed by the headlights of the twenty-first century version of the law that Clifford was driving straight at them. All Sarah's plans for the Hall had crumbled away to nothing. Clifford's claim was secure.

Sarah was out of the Hall. With nothing. Beyond a six-month tenancy agreement on the old tumbledown cottage opposite the Coat. It was a free home, but Cliff was already pushing planning permission through for a new estate, a 'prestigious' development, at the end of the Close. The cottage would go, the bungalow would go, although he was being forced to pay Alan and Flutter a decent price for it.

He wanted The Coat to go, too, but so far the Planning Committee hadn't caved in on that one.

The land was turning out to be very valuable indeed, as Cliff was now getting planning permissions all over the place. And then there were still the remains of the Hall books, pictures and furniture.

Leo hadn't entirely spent the lot. Although not for want of trying.

And Sarah, with no husband, no boyfriend, was pregnant. There seemed to be a polite conspiracy to pretend that this was Leo's child, even though ... Had she needed to have that difficult and embarrassing conversation with Stephan at all? But there had to be a father who was not Derek Maggs.

'Stephan. It's very good of you to agree to this, but ... ' Sarah had tried awkwardly to understand his ready agreement, his not asking who the father really was, her need for a stand-in. 'You see I ... I never meant ... it was such a shock ...'

But he stopped her simply by saying, 'It's the Mrs Maggs problem. I know.'

Amazed and relieved at being so completely understood, she suddenly wanted to confide in him, but he stopped her. 'This is for Anya. She is all that is left. And you are the right one for her. I thank you for it.' He finished his tea and left abruptly, having revealed his feelings in a way he had always been so careful never to do.

Sarah mulled it all over as she walked slowly up the drive. She had cut through the darkening shrubbery, leaves glinting round her as they caught the very last of the sunset. She needed to see the Brats re Anya's stay at their new house, and Flutterby had borrowed the Disraeli Hall Library for a constituency meeting. Clifford was getting as many local groups to the Hall as he possibly could, as they were all future clients for his Hotel and Conference Centre. Alan would be on his chauffeuring duties, running committee members back and forth. She was even hoping to get a lift from him and get in some fish and chips for her and Annie's tea. If Alan would drive them they could go to that really good place on Councillor Betty Smythe Causeway where the cod was so fresh and, most importantly, the portions were so big that one small portion would do for both of them.

She had to make such fine calculations all the time now, and so she was mulling over money, not the mysterious understanding Stephan had shown her, not stairs and darkness, as she approached the dark and apparently deserted frontage of Disraeli Hall.

The bushes still grew tall around the drive and turning circle. And suddenly, quietly, with no particular drama, no sudden change of theme music to warn Sarah, one of the black shrubs detached itself from the others and blocked her path.

At last the darkness at the foot of the stairs had caught up with her. All in black, as black as the cloudy night, it moved in front of her. In the shape of a man. Tall, broad shouldered. Not young. His hand went to the inside of his jacket.

There was no unearthly scream, no

sound at all. Sarah found she had no voice, no movement, no thoughts. There was a crunching on gravel, a rustling. Was this the sound of death, the last sound she would ever hear, the last glimpse she would ever get of this wonderful world? Detachedly, Sarah watched the thoughts clicking through her mind. Death wasn't allowing her time to think about it. She hadn't had enough time; that was all she could manage. Not enough time. Although time, which had been rushing her along faster and faster all her life, now slowed down obligingly, as if it realized she must use the few seconds she had left to the full. Everything had gone into slow motion. She felt the baby tense inside her. She wrapped her hands around her stomach. And now you will never see the world once, Bump. You will know neither feather nor stone. Where did that come from?

'That won't do at all, Squire.' The man

turned and jumped as Alan Brat appeared gruffly out of the dark. 'You're pointing wrong way.' Alan tapped the limo authoritatively. 'You'll want to head back toward Moor if you want to hit motorway for London. If you go on't Tramway you'll ...'

There was a car, parked darkly on the drive. A getaway car. But thank God for it. It had brought Alan Brat out here as surely as the magnets of her faraway school physics lessons had tugged at their iron filings.

Alan was off and away now, the man watching him, his hand frozen inside his jacket. He looked wary and bemused. No Limey Asshole was gonna ... Is that how he would talk, all Philip Marlowish, or what? Why do you suppose he's American, Sarah? He hasn't said anything or done anything yet. Perhaps he was going to break into a Pennies from Heaven type song and dance routine before blazing away. It was all such a theatrical setting. The dark hall, the beam of light from the open door …

Sarah Dexter, will you stop? Pull yourself together! Into the here and now! And do something. This man might have a gun. There are three of us here. She felt her child move inside. Four of us! And without even a catapult to protect us. At any moment he might pull that hand from his jacket and start to blaze away. But as the flow of directions went on, the gunman began to look puzzled, and then, wonderfully, bored. Nobody could actually shoot and kill a fellow human being while they were feeling bored. Nobody.

At that moment he was hit from the right side. 'And I think you'll agree with me that in London …' Flutterby had just arrived, and she never wasted time when there was canvassing to be done. His head spun round, and he fell straight into her hypnotic brown eyes, the enormous lashes right next to his face, as she murmured, 'There is PLENTY of work. PLENTY. So there is NO EXCUSE for any able-bodied young man to–'

She was in white tonight, shining like silver, and her hat was a snowball of white fluff that clung to the side of her silky dark curls. Now he was drowning in her eyes and her heady gardenia perfume.

'I'll just draw it out for you, Squire.' Alan got out the notebook and pen he always kept for these vehicular emergencies and began to write authoritative directions while keeping up a clear and precise commentary. Sarah felt her body unfreeze. The blessed, blessed boringness of the Brats! If she could just quietly fade out of the scene. The only reason this man could possibly have for harming the Brats would be if he shot her in front of them. So, if she wasn't there ...?

Alan, practical as ever, had a large torch, and its radiance lit up his instruction book and all around. If she could just back quietly out of the light, a step at a time, the darkness would swallow her up. She could tiptoe across the lawn and disappear out of range.

It's mad. It's totally mad. Why should anybody want her dead?

Especially now. When she was not the rich young widow after all. When she was not the inheritor of Disraeli Hall and all its speculative building lands.

Another motive for murder moved sharply in her mind. She had to be silenced because she, Sarah Cavalier, could identify the killer! But once again it made no sense. She had seen nothing of the murderer on that terrible night. She had heard footsteps coming slowly up the stairs. She had heard Leo's unearthly scream. And she would hear those things till her dying day. But there was nothing in that to convict anyone.

Which must be why the footsteps stopped. Nobody came upstairs for her after all. If you had got away without being seen, why risk exposure? But it still didn't seem right. As if there was something she wasn't remembering. Some small piece that would cause the whirl of jigsaw pieces in her head fall sharply into place, and cause her to see … What?

Something horrible, something she didn't want to see? She ran over her cast of suspects in her mind. Of course, she couldn't bear to find some tiny piece of evidence that showed it was either of the Brats. But then it wasn't them. How could it be? Anyway, they had just saved her from a hired killer. Hired killer? Now that shrieked Clifford Cavalier Betts. But it was never the obvious person. And anyway, it brought her back to the question of Why. He had got everything he wanted quite legally, and manifestly he relied on his Dream Team, not hired gunmen. Cliff was no fool.

As for Ophelia Plant or the professor? Obviously not.

It always came back to Derek and Ava. But, once again, why? Ava was well in with Clifford, and she'd known before almost anyone that he was likely to get the Hall. But she didn't need to murder anyone. She was better off letting Cliff's legal team do the ousting of Leo and Sarah and the real wife and heir. But Derek, could he have acted autonomously? His motive … he could have had a motive, there was no denying it. Was it possible that Leo and Ava …? Sarah shuddered. She didn't want to think of that. But, a horrible thought: could that moment in the library have been calculated revenge on Derek's part? If so, then it would have been even worse than it already was.

Isn't there anything in my past that I can bear to think about? thought Sarah desperately. Had she made such a mess of her life so far that there was none of it that didn't bring back pain?

But no, he would have gone for Ava

too in that case. She knew that in his own way, he was as possessive of Ava as she of him. And the police would have been on to him like a shot. They always suspected the spouse first, their profession having given them rather a cynical view of marriage. Sarah remembered some fierce questions they had asked her before the lab results came back showing that she had never been near a gun that evening.

And, going with the police view, the other obvious suspects were Donna and her consort. But their alibi checked out. They were on the Awayday weekend, at the Brighton Hotel as they claimed. And were remembered vividly. Apparently Donna spent most of the weekend complaining bitterly about traffic noise and too much light coming in through the curtains of their rather expensive room. She had made it very clear that she was used to a much classier kind of hotel. And the Staff, on being asked to verify their alibi afterwards, had been heard to mutter collectively that it was a pity whoever it was hadn't got that woman too while they were about it.

But who did that leave? Who else did they see? The Mangroves? Debbie and her mum? Maria O'Connell, the hatchet-faced blonde who ran the Home Farm Riding Stables and was Ava's best friend? If Sarah were starring in a Christie, she supposed it would be Debbie; but as she wasn't, she also had to allow there was no way it could have been young Debbie.

A conspiracy by the whole of The Daughters of the Windrush? Councillor Albert Cowlishaw? Surely even the Great Christie herself couldn't make those charges stick?

But somebody had killed Leo. And he was terrified, alarmed, outraged ... outraged when he realized who it was. Sarah realized suddenly that it was a scream of outrage above all else. And

that terrible scream was the only clue
she seemed to have.

* * *

The narrow moorland track was quiet
and dark. And rather muddy. Never
mind, she could find her way back
home with her eyes shut. That was a
smart way to defuse the situation. If it
was a situation. Oh! But wait a
moment! Sarah stopped. Had she done
that foolish thing where the heroine
insists on going down alone into the
creepy old cellar when she realizes the
maniacal killer is in the house?

No. Don't be silly, Sarah, she scolded
herself. If anyone was after her, and he
(or she, she must not forget the
enchanting Ava Maggs) was smart
enough to work out that their hired
killer was going to be ambushed by the
Brats, thus allowing their intended
victim to sneak off across the moorland

track to home, then he (or she) was inescapable anyway. So what was the point of worrying about it?

And why had she been so convinced that the man on the drive was a hired killer? He may have seemed horribly like a piece of the darkness coming to life, but he was most probably looking for Clifford. It was just because he appeared so suddenly. And anyway Alan knew who he was. He knew he was going back to London! I have been a fool, thought Sarah, such a fool. But then she had been so frightened.

The breeze dropped and clouds drifted in a perfect ring away from the moon. Sarah looked up and was caught by the silent beauty of the moorland night sky. It was so dark, and so quiet. And the moon wasn't looking worried for once. It was shining joyfully among its stars.

Is everything going to be all right after all, Moon? Sarah asked it. She only wished it could tell her. It was trying to tell her something, that was for sure. So were the stars, glancing down at her in their joyful shining. They were like a fleet of spaceships dancing across the sky. What were they signalling? What is the Universe? Why? Where did it all come from? There was an infinity of space, an infinity of worlds, and yet she wouldn't even live long enough to explore this wonderful earth. Why? Why did the world end so suddenly for Leo, so young? Was that it then? All he was ever to have?

If an able-bodied man dies, can he live again?

Staring upwards into that infinity of worlds, Sarah stepped off the narrow path and into a rather painful patch of gorse. Watch where you're going, Sarah! And hurry up. If those clouds surge back over the moon, it'll be darker than you can imagine. She scolded herself along the winding path.

It's all wrong, she thought, as she

walked back across the quiet moor. She had been saved by the Brats. Now if this was a Christie, or a Curtiss, or just about any other of the thrillers in the Plants' enormous library, then surely the gorgeous hero would have saved her?

It couldn't end with her walking off into the sunset with Alan and Flutterby Brat. It just couldn't. Although if it did, at least Alan would be sure to know a quicker and better way to get to the sunset. Cheered by the thought, Sarah sang Blue Moon quietly to herself all the way home.

CHAPTER 14

'He'll be out of hospital today, so they tell us. He seemed a bit concussed, so they wanted him to stay overnight.'

Sarah had popped straight round to the Plants to tell Ophelia about last night, but the Disraeli Crescent grapevine, so old and small, still worked well enough. Ophelia knew all about it. In fact she knew more about it than Sarah did. Because the menacing stranger had turned out to be a private detective, hired by Clifford's current ex-wife. She was angling for a better settlement because she had heard he had just become an English milord. And the detective was trying to ascertain the extent of Clifford's staff and property holdings.

Just after Sarah had faded from the scene, Alan had popped back in to get a more detailed map from the library, and, showing surprisingly poor judgment, given his profession, the divorce detective had stopped fishing for his ID and business card, put his arm round Flutterby, and propositioned her with the American equivalent of: 'What's a nice girl like you doing in a place like this?' The handbagging he had received had put him in the local hospital. Flutterby was a woman of severe Victorian values in everything, as befitted her Windrush ancestry. Sarah sat there, drinking her Plant tea, a special herbal concoction the professor insisted on for its calming properties, feeling perhaps that the poor Bump was not getting the start in life that it should. So he hadn't come for her. He was nothing to do with her or Leo. And she had been so scared. So scared. 'Poor Bump,' she patted it ruefully. 'He is going through so much stress it can't be good. My heart jumped into my mouth last night. That idiotic guy just appeared out of the dark. He kind of sprang out at me.'

'Yes, apparently he has been talking to everyone connected with the Hall. Derek even found him poking round the grounds with a torch one night. My dear Sarah, you didn't think ... You don't think someone is trying to kill you!'

'I know. It's ridiculous. Why should anyone? But someone killed Leo, you can't get over that. They were waiting for him. Silently, in the dark at the bottom of our second staircase.' Sarah shuddered and held her stomach protectively. Why couldn't she tell Ophelia about the footsteps coming slowly up the stairs? She couldn't tell anyone about that, she just couldn't. And she didn't know why. 'I shouldn't think or talk about this, Ophelia, not till the Bump appears anyway. I'm getting much too stressed.' She gulped the professorial concoction down hopefully. She really needed something to make her forget. Lethe? Not Rosemary anyway. That was for Remembrance. She must not remember.

'You are quite right, Sarah. We won't talk about it. And don't think about it. I will only say this. The police would be on to it if there was any chance of anything like that. I can't imagine anyone wanting to kill Leo and you.' Ophelia had an old-fashioned faith in the police, one of those fifties things, but Sarah accepted that Ophelia was trying to comfort her.

'No one is trying to kill you, Sarah. No one. You must be sure of that. Your baby needs you to be calm. And anyway it's true. You aren't in any danger.' That was Professor Plant, arriving with further herbal supplies and looking very serious indeed. Sarah felt he had stopped his sentence abruptly and had quickly deleted a 'now' from the end of it.

Which didn't make sense. But then

what did, since the scream and the footsteps? And now Sarah had begun to recognize that something within her didn't want it to make sense.

* * *

The Coat of Many Colours creaked gently on its sign. It had companioned her through many sleepless nights. No matter which way she turned, Sarah couldn't get comfortable. She wondered how it felt from the inside. Was the Bump asleep? Could he hear the Coat creaking? She would have to get up to go to the loo soon anyway, so there wasn't much point going back to sleep. To think she had once planned to have four children!

Yes, and she could check on Anya then, too. Make sure she was sleeping safely in the tiny bedroom that backed on to the Hall grounds. Should she just have left the town? Sarah wondered, not for the first time. People were being very understanding about the Bump; there seemed to be a kind of conspiracy to pretend she was expecting Leo's baby. Her stumbled and unconvincing explanation about her and Stephan had never even been needed. But it would all be so much easier somewhere where she wasn't known. Somewhere that Ava Maggs's sharp eyes didn't penetrate.

But how could she go anywhere at the moment? She must get the birth over with. And she did have a support group here, and somewhere to live. And a job of sorts. Which might continue. There might well be something she could do at the Disraeli Country House Hotel. Something part time that would pay her a little and fit in with school and nursery hours. And she might even be able to stay in the cottage. Maybe Cliff would choose to renovate, not demolish, and keep it as staff accommodation?

She tried not to think of how much

Clifford would get if he redeveloped the Close. And wondered how she, who had once owned her own London flat, seemed about to repeat the difficulties of her own mother. The wind was getting up and the creaking was getting louder. Joseph and his many coloured coat. Many coloured. The colour of bright red blood in the night. And green. Green was the colour of jealousy. Jealousy. Joseph's brothers had been jealous of him. They had thrown him into a pit of darkness. Sarah's thoughts were pulling her back where she didn't want to go, back to the dark at the bottom of the stairs.

Jealousy. Now there was a motive for murder. But why? Who was jealous of who? And why? There was no sense to it. Nobody threw Leo down into the darkness. They shot him. He fell there. And then ...

Well, now she was back to her starting point. Going round and round in the usual circles. It didn't make sense. Donna Cavalier and Prue, they were the heirs. How had they been disinherited so easily? Clifford had a claim, of course, and he had his Dream Team of lawyers. But he also had Ava Maggs.

What had she done? What did she know?

Sarah told herself sharply: I must stop thinking about this. I must. It was as if she was dragging something hidden up to the surface. Something that had better remain hidden. Why didn't the Disraeli Crescenters ever talk about the night of Leo's death, or speculate about the killer? She tried to distract herself with other thoughts. Anya. Her new school. Flutterby's imminent triumph in the Peak Park.

Well, some things were safe. But other things were very dangerous. Certain patterns of thought were going to lead to a horrible conclusion. It was as if the professor's concoction had been the memory herb after all, Plant Rosemary that forced you to remember. Because Sarah felt on the verge of something. Something was going to make sense, something was going to leap out of her subconscious and terrify her. And she was alone here in the night in this old cottage, apart from the tiny sleeping Anya. The part of the mind that never slept was going to let its knowledge float back to the surface, to her consciousness. It would come to her in her sleep, in terrible dreams. You are in no danger NOW, Sarah.

There was danger once, then. And why not now? Did she want to know?

Sarah resolved to stay awake, but already she knew it was too late. Her resolve was almost a dream itself, for it turned out to be a shaky banister at the top of the second staircase that broke as she clutched at it. She felt herself falling into the darkness that had waited at the bottom, where something that she had refused to know until now was going to step out and frighten her to death. She would scream terribly as poor Leo had done, but it would be no use. It was going to tiptoe quietly, quietly up the stairs as it had so many times before, only this time it was going to reach her.

Yes, this time the footsteps hadn't stopped. They continued, coming closer and closer to the door of the bedroom where Sarah clicked and clicked at an empty light switch in the dark. The haunting cry of the hunting owl pulled Sarah back from the edge of dangerous sleep and troubling dreams. She lay in bed shaking, wondering for a moment about the cry that had woken her, before she realized it was the Disraeli Hall owl, an old friend whose calls had punctuated many sleepless nights.

It was the cry of the hunter in the black night.

The cry of the hunter in the black

night! In the dark at the bottom of the stairs.

Sarah sat bolt upright in bed. Quickly, quickly she put the light on. She couldn't face this in darkness. Because she knew now. She knew what she had heard the night of Leo's death. And knowing that, she knew it all. She had heard the cry of the hunter in the dark night. The hunter had cried out. Not Leo. Poor Leo had been dead before he could make a sound, before he knew what had happened to him. Sarah had heard the cry of one taken by surprise as he lurked there, waiting for his victim. And he had saved Sarah. And maybe Anya.

Saved by Boy Tom! She had been saved by Boy Tom.

Of course it was an inhuman cry that she heard. Tom wasn't human. He was beastly. And Leo had trodden on him.

Boy Tom had been lurking around the midnight Hall. As black as night in the black night, he had been crouching on one of the stair treads. And, when Leo came back upstairs with the gun, he trod on him. And fell. And shot himself. And Boy Tom screamed in rage, indignation and hurt pride.

Nobody, but nobody, trod on Tom. It was as simple as that.

And the police knew it. Not about Tom, of course. But they knew, once they had checked her hands for gunshot residue, that it was Leo after her, not some mysterious intruder. And that he had incompetently and incomprehensibly managed to trip and shoot himself instead. They knew that once Leo had shot himself, there was no further threat to his wife and child. What about Anya? Was there ever a threat to her? Could Leo have? Would he have?

She was his own daughter. His only child. He would never shoot his child, she did know that, however unsatisfactory he might have deemed her to be. She knew that as surely as she knew anything. But Sarah? Why? Surely not for that insurance policy. Seventy thousand pounds; that was all, Leo. It covered her mortgage from the flat they had sold for treble that amount. And they had left it running.

Feeling cold and sick, Sarah forced herself to remember truly.

For a start, they didn't 'just leave' the policy, did they? Leo thought it was worthwhile keeping on and paying into and Sarah had agreed and forgotten all about it. Had she actually been pleased to see that he could show a bit of financial foresight after all?

Did Disraeli Crescent know it was Leo? The question startled her. They didn't know about Boy Tom, of course. They probably put the scream down to her vivid imagination, or to owls. The police pathologist must have known Leo couldn't have screamed. He trod on Boy

Tom, and the gun went off. It was a quick death. He would have known nothing, as he knows nothing now.

And it wasn't that she didn't remember. She just hadn't remembered it right.

Something had woken her. Not the scream, not the explosion. But what? Sarah shuddered. She didn't want to remember. But now she had to.

It was dark. Something woke her. And Leo wasn't there. But why did she instantly panic?

Because it was dark? There was no light anywhere. If Leo had got up to go to the loo, there would have been the light on in the hall. The house was so quiet.

Then she heard the scream. And the footsteps. The grandmother's footsteps, coming up the stairs, slowly, slowly, to get her.

And now that didn't make sense. The dead don't walk. So what was she leaving out?

No. She was leaving nothing out. That was what she heard. But she just couldn't admit the sequence of events to herself. Or anyone. Not until now. Because if she had, she would have known who the killer really was. And she couldn't have faced it.

It was the footsteps themselves that had woken her, coming quietly up the stairs, in the pitch darkness.

Someone was trying so hard not to be heard. That was what had wakened her! Don't they say that the subconscious never sleeps? For the first time she was alone with Leo in the Hall at night, and something in Sarah had stayed on guard and woken her.

Then she heard the scream. And the explosion. And they came together. And then that awful silence.

I wonder how and when Boy Tom crept out? she thought inconsequently. And did he have any idea what he had done?

Leo had waited till she was properly

asleep. He had simply switched off her bedside light at the plug. And later someone, not Leo obviously, must have turned it back on. Then he had got his gun from the locked library cupboard. He had tiptoed silently back up the stairs. He had to keep the house dark and quiet. He could face shooting at a dark form in a dark bed, but he couldn't look into her face while he was doing it. Also, if something went wrong, she must not have seen him with the gun.

Could all that kerfuffle he was constantly making about going out on his countryman's pursuits – a'hunting, a'shooting and a'fishing – simply have been a cover? And if so, then he had planned to do this for a long time. Sarah pulled the blankets closer about her but couldn't get warm.

Her heart was fluttering. This couldn't be good for the baby. She was so big now. There was no way of getting comfortable. The birth was looming large, too. And she both dreaded it and longed for it. Just to get it over with. To be comfortable again.

She got up and went quietly downstairs to the cottage kitchen, turning lights on as she went. She had solved the mystery. And nothing more needed to be said. If possible she shouldn't think about it, at least not until the poor Bump was born.

No wonder nothing on her list of suspects had made sense. And no wonder the police had done no more than question her and check her hands for gun residue. She could see now that once they had checked that the insurance policy was on Sarah's life and not the other way round, they were clear enough about the whole business and content to let the Coroner's accident verdict stand. They had more than enough to do.

How did Leo think he could have got away with it? How?

He wasn't usually one to think ahead, that was for sure. But even so. He and his wife are on their own in the house, and his wife is shot. With his rifle. He has a large insurance policy on her life. The police might not have been able to prove anything. Perhaps. But surely at the very least the insurance company wouldn't have paid up.

Unless someone was to provide him with an unbreakable alibi. An alibi that would be brought out with the utmost reluctance, of course. Fancy having to admit that you weren't on holiday with your husband after all, but had taken advantage of his having to go and see a sick mother to ... and with your employer. How reluctantly and blushingly and convincingly Ava could have admitted to that, too. Well, given access to an ocean of blusher, of course.

No. That was something else not to think about. She could never know now. And it didn't signify. All she wanted was

Annie's adoption to be through and the Bump to arrive safely.

The hot cup was comforting and Sarah felt the pounding in her heart calm, and the sick feeling in her stomach subside. She knew it now, as clearly as if she had seen it all. And that was going to prove to be such a relief. The motive was simple and sordid. Money. The murderer was the most obvious one after all. The husband. Or would have been if Boy Tom hadn't intervened.

Her husband. The one she should have been able to trust above all others, the one who was bound to her by their mutual loyal love. What a bleak world it had turned out to be. Poor Bump, to be born into this.

Sarah stopped herself. She must think positively, be positive. Her poor baby, what could he be expecting of the world he was yet to see? It was a miracle he wasn't putting the brakes on and shrinking back to an embryo, instead of growing and apparently thriving. Imagine seeing him for the first time!

Yet she couldn't sit and distract herself by thinking cosy thoughts of the baby who was soon to emerge in place of the Bump. She was terrified he was going to look exactly like Derek. And there was no way she was going to get Annie's adoption safely through before the birth. No way. There was a whole Department of Social Workers to be appeased, forms to be filled in, meetings to be held.

As long as Clifford and the Betts lawyers were on her side, though, Social Services would be scared of her. The Betts lawyers were fearsome. And would sue, departmentally and individually if necessary, whenever any of Cliff's whims weren't met. They had resources behind them that most clients could only dream of.

Ava had done her work well. Although she wasn't quite up to her usual strength at the moment, now Sarah came to think of it. She was looking so haggard these days. She even seemed to have given up on her weight-watching. And she wasn't smoking. Here comes the second shocking revelation of the night, thought Sarah, detachedly. And she couldn't take Valium, not now. Unless she was very much mistaken, Ava Maggs was pregnant.

* * *

The news was officially announced in The Coat of Many Colours the next evening. Ava smiled faintly and took the congratulations as her due. It was clearly all down to her. She had finally decided to get herself pregnant. And so she had, after all these years. It was to be a little girl, apparently. 'I hope she's just like you, Ava,' said Sarah, sincerely and happily. That would serve Derek right, too. He'd be caught between the two of them and ... No, he would play it brilliantly and come out as sleek, happy and well-fed as when he began it.

What grounds do I have for resenting Derek anyway? Sarah asked herself as she felt her brief happiness fading. She was as much responsible as he was. She was hardly poor Debbie, so young and foolish. She knew what she was doing. She could have stopped herself. And, if she told him he was the father of her baby, who knows what he might want to do? Sarah shuddered. That must never, never happen. But he must know, surely? Or is it that he wouldn't want to know, would tell himself that it could be anyone's? He would never want Ava to know, she was certain of that at least. And somehow, Ava's unexpected pregnancy made it even more unlikely that he would ever want to tell her.

She left the Coat quietly and slipped back to her cold little cottage. She wanted to think about the implications of Ava's news. About how it might affect

Annie, herself and young Bump. Ava was obviously very happy about her pregnancy, very absorbed in it, and that would help. Definitely. Her concierge eye wouldn't be as sharp as usual.

But would it now be worse, or better, if she should somehow find out about Sarah and Derek? Sarah had no idea, except that she felt even more strongly that she must never know. In fact this made it imperative that she, Sarah, should leave, as soon after the birth as possible. While the Bump was still a blobby, anonymous baby, the three of them would find a new life somewhere else. Just in case.

Her stomach churned. She must go and find that herbal tea Professor Plant had given her and ... Her thoughts were interrupted by a knock at the door.

* * *

She watched Stephan in a detached sort of way as he read to Annie in his careful, formal English. He ought to be the mystery man coming to take her away from all this, she supposed. He was short, about half an inch shorter than Sarah, with a stocky build. He was really quite ordinary apart from his white-blonde hair. He seemed to have something of the formality of Professor Plant without the professor's lightness of touch and air of romance.

His talk was all of practicalities, too. He did not discuss their arrangement re the fatherhood of her baby. What he felt about all that, Sarah simply did not know; beyond his love for Varya and for her child, he gave nothing away. If only she could have gone the Ava Maggs way and got herself pregnant. But it would take an Ava to carry that off.

They had a coffee before he left, and a stilted little conversation about the maisonette he had bought in East

London. Presumably there would be plenty of work there. He was a computer buff, but not geekish. He was too practical for that.

'I am having a loft-conversion to make a studio.'

'Oh.' Sarah showed polite interest. 'Are you a painter, then?'

'No. I have to work. No time for such things. But it makes a big third bedroom, and I want to do it while I can get the permissions.' Well, that was sensible. You never knew with planners, and he was no Cliff with a legal army behind him. 'No mortgage, we are selling our Warsaw flats. I can do nothing more to my maisonette after this till I save some more. But I am busy in garden.'

To Sarah's surprise he suddenly dropped a file of photos on to the table and started taking her through all stages of his garden. 'This was how it looked when I came.'

Sarah yawned. Although, she had to admit, as the photos came thick and fast and she murmured appreciatively, he really had transformed the little garden. It now had a wall round it, and there was a positively Brat-perfect lawn with fruit trees all about. A practical touch, that.

'Oh. And raspberry canes,' she said politely.

'Ah yes, the professor he gave me those when I first came here.'

'Oh.' She looked at them with more interest. She liked to think of the Plant raspberries going on.

'I can't show you inside yet, though. All is replastered and I have had wiring fixed. But nothing decorated yet.'

Well, that's a relief, thought Sarah, murmuring in what she hoped was a regretful sort of way. She watched Stephan walk stolidly down the path towards the Plants' and wondered yet again about him and Varya. She could see why Leo swept her off her feet, she really could. All that charm. Poor Stephan doesn't have an ounce of it.

But was it wise? Varya, might you and your daughter have done better to make a different choice? What had there been under that charm, that lethal charm?

Thinking of children seemed to have triggered something, disturbed the child inside her.

What awful things she had been thinking, thought Sarah remorsefully. That dreadful, dreadful night. At least now it was sorted out in her mind, so could she not stop obsessing and stop fearing? Even though her own husband had tried to murder her?

But she would never forget. And how could she ever think of marrying again, after that?

She murmured to the child within her, 'It's probably better for you that I don't, little Bump, as so often stepfathers aren't the best option.'

Oh! A sharp, sudden pain, as if something irrevocable had happened inside her. She sat down for a moment, clutching at her middle. She had better go up and get that carefully packed suitcase, as the Bump was only ten days from his date, and it was possible he was not going to wait any longer. Though they say that first babies are always late, she reassured herself. And it's not as if there was any chance that she had the conception date wrong. If only.

Sarah set off slowly up the narrow cottage stairs, doubling over as another, larger pain hit her amidships. Panicking, she clutched for the banister. But suddenly there was nothing. No rail. No pain. No stairs under her feet. Nothing. Just emptiness and silence.

CHAPTER 15

The next thing was blackness, the blackness of darkness. And someone was struggling through it. Is it me? wondered Sarah. But who was 'me'? A nebulous concept that couldn't quite be grasped. Someone was having a very difficult time of it.

'You don't want to go that way, Squire. You'll find head first is better.' That was Alan. Ah, he was drawing the route. Good old Alan. That will help ... the struggler ... Me ...? Us?

And Flutterby was waiting. She had a sheaf of job applications with her. FOR ALL ABLE-BODIED YOUNG MEN, they said, in large bold print. So that was all right. He was able-bodied. Keep going, keep going, whoever you are.

For they were in trouble. They had to get to the Plant kitchen somehow. Ophelia leaned forward tensely as the

Weathergirl began to point to her large chart. Stormy weather, stormy weather, stormy weather ...

'I always like a womb with a view.' Ophelia laughed heartily, but the big stone windows showed them icy wind whirling the professor's cloak. Trees crashed around him, their leaves raining down. Chicken feathers swirled round his sword. He was fighting for his chickens. There was a fox out there somewhere. Waiting. It smiled so charmingly, but its eyes were ice.

It was so cosy in the Plant kitchen. So safe, so warm. Why did they have to leave? All the dangers were outside. All the stormy weather. Held back by the valiant Plant.

You must. Or I must. We must. Into the lonely world. With no loyal love anywhere to be found. Who do I love? And who loves me? It is all leaving you. It's gone. You can't keep it. You must leave.

Nearly there. Just keep going.

'Straight ahead, Squire.' That was Alan's gruff voice. Flutter rustled her application forms eagerly. But – Oh no. Now Derek had appeared. Smiling slyly. And Ava, hot on his trail. They would never escape from the trap. They will be waiting for us ... For you? For who? But all the struggles will have been in vain. Professor Plant sprang forward, cavalier feathers fluttering, sword at the ready. The sword would save her. Us. The strugglers. The sword slash.

Sarah looked desperately up at Flutter's hat. It was so bright and cold and big that she couldn't see her face. Even the enormous eyes were dimmed.

But it was a light. A bright flat light shining down from a white ceiling. Why was Flutter's hat on the light? Why was she in bed in the Plant kitchen? And wouldn't someone turn that light off?

'Able-bodied?' Was that my question, wondered Sarah, or did it belong to Flutter?

'Yes, everything is fine, dear. Don't worry. He's fine. You have a lovely son.'

Oh no. Now this was a hospital nightmare. Sarah shut her eyes. But someone was holding her hand. The hands, joining, felt real and concrete. They were pulling her back to something. She opened her eyes again, and, with an effort, turned her head. Stephan. He was sitting there holding her hand tightly.

'Good afternoon,' he said stiffly. 'I found you on the floor. At the bottom of the stairs.' After a pause, he said quietly, 'I am the official father, if you remember. It's expected that I should be here and hold your hand.'

Sarah sat up. Or tried to. It hurt. Her stomach felt both flatter and swollen. And painful.

'The baby. My baby.'

'He's fine, Sarah. They are bringing him now.'

And Sarah found herself holding a tiny white parcel. She stared at a small face. It was pale and tired. But calm. The face stared at her.

'Is that you, Bump?' It looked like it was.

Stephan looked dutifully at the transformed Bump. The nurse smiled down at them.

He got up and made a little formal bow. 'Yes, We have a beautiful son. I thank you very much.' The thanks seemed to be directed both at Sarah and the nurse. Don't overplay your part, Stephan. Sarah felt grateful he was there, but she just wanted to be on her own and think about, and realize, what had happened. On her own with this new little being.

'Where did Ophelia go? And the prof ...' Her voice tailed off as she realized they were all part of her dream. And so, thankfully, were Derek and Ava.

'He has blue eyes, just like you.' Then

she remembered that all babies had blue eyes.

I needn't have asked him to do this, she thought ruefully, after all Derek and Ava would be gone very soon. Still, it had to be safer. Even though she could see no look of Derek in him. The transformed Bump simply looked like a baby, and completely himself. Although, as Sarah looked more closely, she noticed that he was also the most beautiful baby there had ever been.

Yet it would only take one baby photo ... Just suppose he turned out to be the spitting image of the Baby Derek! He was not going to be like his father, though. Not in most ways. Because she would really love him.

I do really love him, thought Sarah, surprised, looking down at the wrinkly face of her Bump. He looked a bit thoughtful and puzzled. As well he might. It was a wonder the poor little soul had been in a hurry to enter this frightening new world. The glimpses he had got from the womb couldn't have been very encouraging.

'He looks very neat.' Apart from the wrinkly worried forehead, he seemed as pressed and polished as the Brat garden.

'We had to do a caesarean, dear. You've just woken up.'

'They had time for a wash and brush up.' And that was Ophelia just arriving on the other side of her! I didn't dream her after all. Sarah was amazed.

'He wasn't looking quite so polished and pressed when he emerged. Poor little soul was the wrong way round and everything. He had been struggling for a long time before Stephan found you. If he hadn't arrived when he did! He'd left one of his photo albums and just popped back across the road to get it. Thank goodness you hadn't locked your front door, Sarah. He found you lying at the bottom of the stairs, bleeding badly. Plant rang for the ambulance.

Which was encouraging, as he has been getting so confused lately. Although I think the ambulance crew were a bit surprised to be told it was me who was having the baby when he opened the door to them.'

The professor. With his sword! He had saved her. The ashes of Disraeli Crescent had sent up one last golden flame.

'We locked everything up behind us. So don't worry. The cottage will be safe.'

Sarah smiled weakly. All the treasure she had was here, on the bed with her. She couldn't even hold the little bundle. He was propped up somehow. But she knew what she had to say. Ava Maggs was vividly in the offing. 'Steven. We'll call him Steven.'

Something jolted: foxes, chickens. Both my chicks! Great danger. 'Anya. Where is Anya?'

'She's with Alan and Flutter, dear. Don't worry.'

At which point Sarah either fell asleep

or lost consciousness, and everything stopped for a while.

* * *

'Now. You must take it easy. They were only just in time, you know. And that was an operation you just had. It's good the baby has a father around who is going to help.'

The almoner sighed. That so often wasn't the case nowadays.

The snow lay thick outside and Sarah clutched Steven protectively to her as the shock of the cold hit her. The cottage is going to be so cold, young Bump. I hope you are tough 'un. Snow so early! What was happening to the weather in this new century? The Plants must be bursting with the excitement of the new millennium's forecasts.

'We shall be on our own, you and I. And Anya. It's the three of us against the world from now on.' Young Steve slept placidly through his mother's worries. Stephan had gone back to his maisonette. He had talked quite a lot about paint colours and then, rather awkwardly said his goodbyes. Well, he had been a good friend for a short time. He had put his name on Steven's birth certificate. Did he realize the implications of that? Of how he could be got at for maintenance? If Sarah had to go on the dole at any stage, and she couldn't see how it was to be avoided, she was going to have to say that he had gone back to his country. And she didn't have an address for him.

It wouldn't even be a lie as that was exactly what he had done. He and his brother were finalising the sale of the last of their converted flats in Warsaw. And she had taken care not to have an address, either for London or for Poland.

Poor Leo. What he could have done with Disraeli Hall if he had had a bit of ...

Sarah didn't finish the sentence

because of the cold chill the word 'Leo' brought in its train. He had wanted to kill her. To finish her life, there and then, in the middle of the night. For 70,000 pounds.

'That'll be seven pounds, seventy pee, love,' the taxi driver said, startlingly. She paid it over. Even adding a small tip. My last taxi, she thought as she watched him drive gingerly back down the snowy Crescent. She was going to be hard pushed to afford bus fare from now on.

Now for Anya, who had been farmed out again. Although she was quite happy to stay with Willoughby and Harrington. Sarah would pick her up tomorrow morning and she could meet her new brother.

When she asked about her father later, Sarah was going to have to say the right thing. Not praise him to the skies or anything like that. But she could always truthfully say how handsome and charming he was. And how sad it was he died so young. And Sarah would have to lie a little and say how much he loved her. Because that is how it should have been. Every little girl must be loved by her father as well as her mother. I think somehow she will know how much Varya loved her. It will be in the fabric of her being, programmed in from birth, when mother and daughter first set eyes on each other.

Sarah would never tell her about ...

No. Just stop it, Sarah. This was to be a new life, a new beginning. She fumbled at the new front door. She must get young Steve in quickly. It really was cold. Winter had arrived suddenly during her hospital stay.

She was glad once again that Steve was not Leo's. How to tell a child that his father was a murderer? But whatever was she to do about Steve and his father? He would have to have a father. He would have to know the truth.

And yet, how could she ever safely tell him? When? What if he took off for Australia, where the Maggs trio were apparently going to settle, as soon as he was old enough? What if he never forgave her? Surely he was entitled to a father's love, a father's presence? But, if she owned up, then what?

Do what thou wilt shall be the whole of the law. And yet what an impossible, heart-rending mess it left behind, when you did what you wilt, regardless.

CHAPTER 16

Another Spring. And, appropriately, it was a sad and rainy one. Perhaps Sarah's last Spring in the town of grey stone walls. Where was she going to go? What were they going to do?

Sarah listened listlessly to the radio. Or wireless, as the Plants would have it still. The TV had had to go. She simply couldn't afford the licence fee. The news was much as ever, the usual trouble spots giving trouble, the usual Peace Agreements falling apart, and another train had crashed. Oh, and all the kingdoms of the world were, yet again, going to bring about world peace. Mainly it seemed by bombing each other. Altogether, the new millennium was proving very like the old.

The media had long given up on Councillor Cowlishaw, although the world's scientific community was still united in its frenzy of translation, making a small oasis of unity and co-operation in a fractured world.

They didn't hear much of Flutterby on the local news now that she was a Peak Park MP. But Councillor Betty Smythe was on. She was not as glamorous, but every bit as forceful. Even so, she was having to bow to the people's choice and leave office. Though she bravely assured the camera she was going to be fine. She had a new career awaiting. She was going to be the first to bring the VCA Franchise to the town. She was going to open the Victorian Cake Anchor Emporium; Kitchenalia R Us. The first of many, she sincerely hoped.

Sarah felt robbed. She had thought the Victorian Cake Anchor to be her very own invention, and now they had taken it out of her head and franchised it. And after all, who needed the money more, her or Ex-Councillor Betty Smythe?

There is nothing new under the sun,

though, she consoled herself. All our 'inventions' were copied from nature anyway. The Creator had done it all first. And done it better, and always more beautifully. Undoubtedly there was some kind of animal out there that had a built-in VCA. Sarah tried to distract herself from her worries by wondering what sort of creature it might have been, and what on earth it would have wanted a Cake Anchor for. But it was no use. Feelings of sadness and desolation threatened to overwhelm her. She felt so alone in the world.

She couldn't say she had been left with nothing. Never! She had a son and a daughter. Young Steve was proving to be a happy and sunny baby, so far unscarred by the turmoil of his mother's womb. Quickly, quickly he had forgotten the anxieties of his first nine months, the wrinkly forehead had been ironed out, and his face had become a smooth piece of silk for life to write on. Annie was nobody's daughter now if she wasn't Sarah's, and the adoption was finalized at long last. The very instant it was through, Sarah had been advised that her services at the library were no longer required. It turned out they were required for Debbie, who had never annoyed Ava in any way. But Sarah had Annie, which was all that mattered. She did not forget her pledge to Varya. She couldn't help but wonder more and more about that late night drive on the ice. What had Varya found out? Was she leaving Leo? Was he chasing after her?

He had refused to give Donna a divorce. What might he have felt when another partner said she was leaving?

Now that she was free, Donna and Shug were married. Prue had sulked off to Roedean, which must be costing somebody. And the Maggses had already taken flight to Australia, with young Maubretia. Who was neither a copy of Ava nor Derek, but completely herself.

And she looked fully capable of rising above her name.

They had done well out of everything. They had bought a bed and breakfast Hotel in Cairns. Or at any rate, it had been bought for them. The Coat had even received a postcard showing a dramatic bit of garden, ablaze with exotic birds and spiky plants. Clifford had certainly paid for getting enmeshed with Ava. She had been a match even for his lawyers. Yet she seemed to have felt the need to move her spoil a long way away. You could hardly get further than Australia. Or was there some other reason for taking herself and Derek far away from the grey stone town where Benjamin Disraeli had once spent an eventful weekend? Was it Derek she wanted to get away safely?

If Sarah had had the time to think it out, and to do her history homework, she had a depressing feeling that in the relationship, politics and treaties of

Clifford Cavalier Betts and Ava Maggs she would find a disturbing miniature of the larger politics of the world, with its temporary alliances, its breakable treaties, its infallible instinct for picking on the weak and vulnerable, for knowing who mattered and who didn't.

Anyway, Cliff had the Hall. It was his and unencumbered. He had five sons in all, mostly from his earlier American marriages. So Disraeli Hall had its dynasty. Although as it was now The Benjamin Disraeli Country House Hotel, Sarah supposed it could be said that the Dynasty no longer had its Hall.

Cliff had moved back down to the Home Counties and commuted between his palace there and a Penthouse flat close to Sloane Square. Plans and pictures of both residences had been floating around for some time, and Sarah had to admit they were charming. In fairness, there was nothing of Southfork about the mansion. All was in subdued good taste. He and his wife and young Benjamin Cavalier Betts wouldn't half rattle about in it, though. His other children were all grown up and had no interest in living outside of the U.S. of A.

And I am leaving Disraeli Crescent, thought Sarah sadly, as she watched the tulips shining after the rain. The cottage was to be demolished as part of the redevelopment. So here she was. Alone with Anya and tiny Steve. All three soon to be homeless.

* * *

Sarah was all they had in the world. And the children were all she had in the world. How did we get so lonely and so separated? she wondered. And she thought once again of Disraeli Crescent in its Fifties heyday. She could have managed then. There was a support group right here on the road. All the young mums, and the children playing safely outside …

What made them throw it away? A community of mothers supporting each other: was it as idyllic as it sounded? Or was it just that the horrors of the past fade, and only what is good gets remembered?

Professor Plant had pointed out that whatever else was true, the Fifties ended up right here, right now. So they must have contained the essence of their own destruction. Was everything futile, then? Was all endeavour to come to nothing? Something in Sarah said No. That there was something real, something worth striving for. If only she could find it. It was as if there was a big question standing there. And if only Sarah could see what it was, she might be able to find the answer.

One of the household appliances pinged suddenly, startling her. The washing machine. The endless cycle of washing, drying, hanging out, ironing, putting away. That needed to be attended to. And just remember, Sarah scolded herself, when you get too soaked in nostalgia for a past you didn't even know, there were no washing machines then. Two tiny children. No washing machines. Not even a fridge. She could remember Ophelia lamenting having disposed of her washboard set, given that they were now quite valuable antiques. Washboarding the clothes! That must have been hard work. And she used to mangle things, not spin and tumble them. The mangle had survived in a rusty way until the day of the move when Sarah had seen it lying sadly in the big skip outside no. 5.

Yet Disraeli Crescent had blazed into life one more time to save her. The Crescent had nurtured Boy Tom, an unregenerate cat of the Fifties, no collar, all his own claws; and, like Sir Galahad, he had charged over to the Hall and fought and slain the dragon.

If Sir Tom the Terrible hadn't been lurking there that night, she would now be in that cemetery, so high up, where the cold winds blow in from the moor. The world would be going on without her. And there would be no Steve anywhere in it. And what of Anya? Where would she be?

And it was Stephan, the visitor at No. 5 Disraeli Crescent, who had saved her and young Steve when she had fainted on the stairs. He would be the last visitor, as it turned out.

* * *

Because now Disraeli Crescent was leaving her. As if, angry at being swept so clinically from his Hall, Benjamin D was taking his Crescent with him.

Joseph and his Coat of Many Colours no longer creaked reassuringly on the signboard during the nights. A phallic new sign proclaimed 'The Jolly Sausage', part of the 'Winkles Seafood N Champagne' chain. It was presided over by The Real Mrs Cavalier, Donna. Who was not especially jolly, but did have personality plus. Shug, her dour consort, reigned there too. Presumably he was satisfactory in the sausage department as he appeared to have nothing else to recommend him. With none of the nous of Ava Maggs, Donna appeared to have been fobbed off with only the tenancy of The Sausage, although someone was paying for pouting Prue's fancy schooling.

The Sausage had strong competition from Dizzies, the wine bar that now occupied the old servants' quarters of Disraeli Hall. The noise from its karaoke nights would have drowned out the gentle creaking of the Coat of Many Colours anyway, Sarah supposed.

The round gatehouse was already

covered in scaffolding, undergoing its conversion into yuppie – or whatever the twenty-first century equivalent was going to be – studio flats.

The Brat bungalow stood empty. Bought by Clifford, it awaited demolition. Now that Flutterby had swept to power in the Peak Park, the Brat notepaper proclaimed: The Old Mill, at Stone. Annie had been very excited to see Uncle Alan, Auntie Flutter, Willoughby and Harrington on the BBC News one evening.

Sarah and the children sometimes went over to Stone on Sunday afternoons. The Old Mill had a tiny stream running through the garden, which kept Annie, Wills and Harry completely occupied. So the grown-ups were able to talk, while young Steve slept his baby sleep, unaware that the world wasn't fresh and new, waiting with bated breath for his arrival so that it could begin.

They had met up, too, at the Nursing Home where Professor Plant was revisiting all his early days; sometimes he lay in lupin meadows in Poland, dazed with the honey scent; sometimes he searched for a young Ophelia, laughing in her clouds of dark hair; sometimes he clutched at Annie, calling her Emily, and holding her tight.

No. 5 was being converted into student flats. Mrs Plant was living with her eldest son and his family. They lived within the radius of Boy Tom territory, otherwise the move simply wouldn't have been feasible. She and the boys visited the professor every day; and Sarah, Annie and the Brats shared the weekends. They had decided to phone Emily and she was said to be flying home.

Sarah's little cottage would be demolished as soon as Clifford's lawyers got her out of it.

The Close was going to be re-developed together with the formal gardens that Clifford had sold off. It was going to be a rustic village development, a 'prestigious' development, a mixture of mellow brick and stone. It was going to be quite pretty, actually, with all its trees designed in. But it wouldn't be something that Sarah, Annie and young Steve could afford.

Whatever are we going to do? What happened to all my plans, to everything? Why can't I rid myself of the feeling that the long arm of the Cavaliers is somehow going to reach out and grab Anya from me? These and other questions tormented Sarah night and day, but above all she wondered how to get rid of this horror, that someone had planned to kill her, so coldly, so deliberately. The one she trusted.

Sometimes she felt that all she had to hold on to was what Stephan had told her when she had voiced something of her night fears to him. He had startled her by getting out a Bible and reading carefully from it words that had become something of a mantra. 'As for the dead, they are conscious of nothing at all.' They can't come back and get you. Sarah felt he had known from the start just why Varya was driving so fast that night, and exactly who had been coming up the stairs with a gun in his hand.

'Uncle Step! Uncle Step!'

Annie, are you reading my mind? Sarah looked over to the little bay window where Annie was sitting, colouring in her spring flower picture. She liked to have everything just so and was studying the late daffodils and tulips while sorting through her yellow and orange crayons.

'Uncle Step!' She pressed her face against the window. And there was Stephan coming up the path. He was laden down with an enormous ethnic rag doll, which looked much too good to be played with. He also had a gigantic

Mothercare bag and a bunch of Spring flowers. Freesias.

Stephan! What was he doing here? Had he come to visit 'his' son? How correct of him, if so! She went to wave him round the back of the cottage because the front door had swelled shut with all the rain and was immovable. But he saw Annie waving and rushed over to the window. Sarah had forgotten how sunny his smile was. It transformed his face. He hadn't smiled much when he was last here, but then she supposed there hadn't been much to smile about.

Sarah got up to let him in the kitchen door, and stopped. Frozen. Annie and Stephan. Stephan and Annie. Their faces pressed close together, only glass separating them. Ash blonde hair, navy blue eyes, honey skin. Smiles of surprising sunniness. Like reflections in a mirror. Here was a whole sub-plot she had never even suspected.

Poor Leo, not only didn't he have any

sons; he only had the one daughter, the sullen Prue. And perhaps not even her. Could he have quite cynically married Varya, knowing ... or had she ... No wonder Stephan ...

But he had come back to be with Annie. His Anya. He loves her. And he hasn't left her.

Slowly, as if in a dream, Sarah went to the kitchen door. Stephan. He's come back for young Steven too. And for me.

She suddenly remembered the photo albums. The maisonette, the extra room, the little garden, all carefully fenced in, with lots of lawn. A warm feeling began to curl round the desolate feeling in her heart. Had there been someone out there in the cold, empty world thinking of them, making a home for them? Yes. That is why he came round with the photos. That is why ...

'How did she know that?' was followed by the questions: Can we ...? Could we ...?

What a strange family they would be. Father, mother, son and daughter. The perfect pigeon pair. Their daughter, their adopted child, the world would suppose. Yet who was actually his daughter. And his adopted son, who would be his real son in the eyes of the world. At least there would be no need for any more dealings with the Social. Stephan's name was on Steve's birth certificate, and he was Annie's father.

And he would care for them both. They would care for them both.

What a muddle they had made of that clear and loyal and lovely arrangement that God had set in place in the Garden of Eden. But there was no one else in the world who would care for Steve and Annie as they would. As they did. Could they make this work? For the children's sake? After all, thought Sarah, I have tried the romantic road to marriage and it couldn't have worked worse. This would be an arranged marriage, a marriage arranged by the needs of two children who we both love.

She opened the door. The rain had finally stopped and Spring sunlight burst in with Stephan. They stared at each other, speechless, the scent of freesias filling the space between them.

Boy Tom simmered in his guest basket by the fire. Annie danced excitedly at Stephan's legs. 'Come and see our baby, Uncle Step!'

All the commotion woke Steve up. His eyes lit on Stephan. He beamed. 'Now,' his round fresh face said. 'Now the world begins.'

The End

If you have enjoyed this story, please leave a review for Sue to let her know what you thought of her work.

Also by Sue Knight

Waiting for Gordo

'Hidden depths – the story has an unsettling dream-like quality that gets to you.'

Till They Dropped
– also available as an audio short.

'A perfect gem of a story that comes satisfyingly full circle yet ends on a shiver.'

You can find out more about Sue on her author page on the Fantastic Books Store. While you're there, why not browse our delightful tales and wonderfully woven prose?

www.fantasticbooksstore.com

Printed in Great Britain
by Amazon

47153368R10165